the trouble with you is

FIRST SERIES : SHORT FICTION

# the trouble with you is

*and other stories*

Susan Jackson Rodgers

MID-LIST PRESS

*Minneapolis*

Printed in the United States of America.

**Library of Congress Cataloging-in-Publication Data**
Rodgers, Susan Jackson, 1960-
    The trouble with you is : and other stories / by Susan Jackson Rodgers.
        p. cm. – (First series–short fiction)
    Contents: Women of will – How I spent my summer vacation – The two husbands
– Fits and starts – Bust – Luck – Bones and flowers – Delivery – Remembering Tom
Blake – Beautiful things – Lost spirits – Green beans – The rice in question – The
trouble with you is – Still life.
    ISBN 0-922811-60-1 (trade paper original : alk. paper)
    1. United States – Social life and customs – Fiction.  I.  Title.  II.  Series.
PS3618.O356T76  2004
813'.6–dc22                                                         2004000960

First printing 2004

Earlier versions of the some of these stories appeared the following periodicals: *Beloit
Fiction Journal* ("Fits and Starts," "How I Spent My Summer Vacation"); *Nimrod*
("Bones and Flowers" published as "Desert Life"); *Prairie Schooner* ("The Trouble
with You Is"); *StoryQuarterly* ("The Rice in Question"); *The Chariton Review*
("Remembering Tom Blake"); *Willow Review* ("Women of Will").

*For my mother and father,*
*and in memory of my brother,*
*Peter Blackwood Jackson (1956–1994)*

# contents

# acknowledgments

Thanks to Marianne Nora, Lane Stiles, and Mary Logue at Mid-List Press. For financial assistance and for affirmation that came at crucial times, many thanks to the Kansas Arts Commission. Much appreciation, too, to the literary magazine editors who have published my stories. Family, friends, and colleagues have been a tremendous source of encouragement and support over the years, and I am grateful to you all.

Most profound gratitude and love to the dearest children in the world—Samuel, Margaret, and Benjamin—and to my husband, Larry: best reader, best friend, best everything.

# women of will

It's just coincidence, I guess, that the three of us happen to be standing around the hors-d'oeuvres table together when Will arrives at the party with his new lover. This is the downside of living in our picturesque college town: sooner or later you bump into every man you ever dated or slept with or married. In the case of Will, you probably bump into him often, and he is probably with his new girlfriend.

"Well, well, lookee here," Cecilia says. It's Cecilia and Maryanne and I around the food table. We don't know each other well, but tonight we feel for the first time our common bond. We watch as our hostess welcomes the latecomers, and we wear ironic smiles as Will removes his lover's coat from her petite frame, leaning into her to whisper something. He drapes the coat over his arm and carries it off like treasure to the guest room, where all our coats are piled on the bed. He hasn't looked our way yet, but she has. And quickly away again. Her face and throat flush a deep shade of red.

"Who is she?" I ask. "She looks familiar." We're far enough away, and the party is already loud enough, that I know she can't hear me.

"Julie," Cecilia says. "Julie from the college bookstore. She's in textbooks, I think." Cecilia knows everyone, and since she and Will broke up over two years ago, she's the one most enjoying this spectacle. Maryanne's decidedly not. She has become rigid, gripping her wine glass and holding her head in a way that tells me her haircut is new, and she isn't sure if it becomes her. It does become her, and I want to tell her she looks pretty, but I don't want her to think I feel sorry for her. Which I do. After all, Julie is Maryanne's successor. The first time out is never easy.

I'm somewhere in between. Will and I broke up about a year ago. We met when Will, who is a freelance writer, was doing a piece on the college art museum, where I coordinate special events—lectures, readings, receptions for new exhibits. He interviewed me on a Monday afternoon. By Monday night we had a date. By Friday night I was thinking, maybe he's the one. He wasn't, obviously. Now when I see him, my heart still pounds too hard. You can't help that, can you? A pounding heart. And yet I think I'm almost over it. I think I'm very, very close.

"You think he'd begin to develop some sense of shame," I say.

"Or move on to the next town," Cecilia says.

Maryanne doesn't say anything. She gulps the rest of her wine and keeps her eyes on Julie, who stands in the entryway, her hands folded in front of her like a schoolgirl waiting to be called on. Then Will reappears and guides her, his hand on the small of her back—we can all feel it there—toward the kitchen for drinks. Guides her right through the dining room, where we stand waiting. There is a moment, a truly wonderful moment, when Will finally looks up and sees us as he passes, and sees who we are—the last two years of his life flashing before him like a semaphore. The tiniest shift in his expression reveals his momentary panic, but he is still Will. He quickly recovers. He smiles vaguely at each of us, as if we are distant cousins, people he met a long time ago at a family reunion that he didn't particularly want to attend. The coffee-brown eyes take us in, and release us, one at a time: "Hi Maryanne. Hi Celia, hi Beth." And then he adds softly, to Maryanne, "Your hair looks nice." Maryanne doesn't move, doesn't even breathe.

Cecilia saves her. "So what's new with you, Will?"

He smiles over his shoulder—he's already pushing the swinging door of the kitchen, getting Julie away from us as quickly as possible—"Oh, you know. Same ol', same ol'." I can't tell if he's trying to be funny or self-deprecating. The door swings shut behind them.

"I think he really means, the more things change, the more they stay the same," I say.

"I can't handle this," Maryanne says.

"More wine," Cecilia answers, taking Maryanne's glass to the now-forbidden zone of the kitchen, and returning with it a moment later full. Under one arm she's carrying an unopened bottle of Chardonnay, and when she motions with her chin to follow her, we do, single file, into the back bedroom where the coats are, as if we've had a rendezvous with each other all evening, as if this is why we came to the party in the first place.

Cecilia and I push the coats into a pile on the floor and sit on the bed, cross-legged. Maryanne sits on the floor, leaning against the coats. I notice Will's on top, a heavy black overcoat whose woolly male smell I can still recall, though I don't care to, at the moment. He wore the coat on our last date together. I suppose you could say we broke up that night, though the specific words were never said.

"If he could just get us all into one body, then maybe he'd be happy," Maryanne says now. We laugh, because we are all so different-looking, an assortment of possibilities, like a sampler box of chocolates: Will has taken one bite out of each of us, then decided to try something else. With Maryanne it was the jade-green eyes he went for, the hint of Asian blood that gives her face an exotic cast.

Cecilia—well, as we used to say in high school, Cecilia is stacked. Big round happy breasts and bottom, full lips, highlighted hair. Not his type, but then who is? Theirs was a quick affair, all about sex, or so he told me. "We did it like rabbits," he reported. As if I really wanted to know.

I'm the tall skinny one, with enough Italian on my mother's side to give me skin that tans to a deep coppery brown with only a few hours in the sun. It's probably no coincidence that Will and I started dating in early summer, and broke up the next winter. When I felt him losing interest, I had this terrible urge to run to a tanning salon. Even now I catch myself wondering if it would have helped. (Then I remind myself about the trip to Florida, how I flew down there when things started going bad between us, how I came back with a gorgeous tan, and how we broke up anyway.)

"The trouble with Will," Cecilia says now, and we listen to her as if this is a lecture we have paid admission to hear, "is that he grew up with four sisters. A twin sister even. He's used to women adoring him."

"He's a jerk, that's the trouble with Will," Maryanne says, tears making her eyes even shinier and brighter than before.

"The trouble with Will," Cecilia says again, opening the wine bottle with a corkscrew she produces from her blazer pocket, "is that he knows how to talk girl talk. His sisters taught him how. But he's dealing in an emotional currency whose value he isn't equipped to understand." Her red fingernails flash like sparks as she tops off our glasses with the wine. "He spends this currency extravagantly. He gets you very close to him, very fast, because he knows how to do it. He's not manipulative. He doesn't realize what he's doing. He just knows it makes us feel good. And when we feel good—"

"—he feels good," I say.

"Right. You are led to believe you are something special. And you know what? You are something special. For a while anyway. I'm not saying he's lying. I'm not saying he's a bad person. He just has a very short attention span."

"Meanwhile," I say, "you start thinking, My god, this is it. This is the guy. This is the one guy on the planet who completely understands me."

"A best friend with a penis," Cecilia says.

"You're a lot smarter than he gave you credit for," I tell her.

"We all are, honey."

"He made me feel smart," Maryanne says. "I felt like my best self with him."

That shuts us up for a moment. Because it's true. Will has that power: to make you feel like your truest, best self. During our ten months together I did things I had never done before, but always meant to—took a pottery class, went kayaking. I even kept a journal. It embarrasses me to read it now, and embarrasses me even more to recall the time I read excerpts out loud to Will. He ate it up, of course—all the early, intense feelings recorded in horrifying detail. I vow to myself to throw it out as soon as I get home tonight. And to start a new one that begins with this exact conversation, and then never mentions Will again.

"I was obsessed with him," I say now, thinking of all those pages filled with such over-the-top yearning, like an adolescent. "It was disgusting. What was that about, do you suppose?"

"He's great in bed," Cecilia admits.

"I used to think he was the Devil," I say. "I had myself convinced. I don't mean figuratively the devil. I mean the Devil himself." I pause for a moment as two women in their twenties, whom I recognize from my lunch-hour aerobics class, come into the room. We take their coats as if we've been assigned to the job, and crack a few jokes. I notice Maryanne putting their coats to the side, so that Will's is still on top of the pile. Oh dear, I think, but I let it go.

I get back to my story. "Sometimes when we were in bed, I'd look up at his face, and his hair, which was pretty long then, would fall into these clumps on the sides of his head, and I'd think, my god, he has horns. Those clumps looked like small horns. His eyes … burned. I thought he was stealing my soul."

They nod, considering for a moment. "That's possible," Cecilia says. "The Devil theory would certainly explain the violent feelings I had after we broke up. Directed toward you," she says to me. "I hated you! Will and I had barely split up, and there you were, already on the scene. I used to see you with him at the Café Allegro—my store is across the street—and I wanted to go in there and pour hot latte all over your skinny self." She shakes her head.

"Don't feel bad. I hated you, too. I kept comparing the two of us. I kept thinking, there's no way he can't be comparing us, and finding me … lacking." I glance at her cleavage.

"But then you figured, he chose me. He chose *me*," Cecilia says.

"Right. But then he chose you," I say to Maryanne. "And I really hated you. There you were with those eyes, and that smile, and I wanted to smash your face in." I shrug an apology.

"So much for sisterhood," Cecilia says.

Maryanne laughs in this sweet way that makes me wonder why Will left her. Then she asks Cecilia, "So who came before you?"

"Oh, there's a long history of Will's women! We have an illustrious past. There should be a course offered, Will 101. Advanced Will. How to Be a Woman of Will." She smiles.

"A woman of will, I like that. That sounds strong."

"It is. We are a strong people. We have been filled with Will and now we are—willful."

"So before you?" Maryanne asks again.

Cecilia takes a deep breath and tells us about Kathy, and then about a woman named Faye or Faith—Cecilia can't quite remember which—and then about Wendy, Jill, and Kara. That is as far back as she can go. As Cecilia's talking, I notice something strange. Maryanne is fingering the leather buttons on Will's coat. Her hands start crawling into his pockets like furtive animals. Cecilia's watching, too, but we don't say anything. I take the wine and top everybody off, which kills the bottle. I'm hoping maybe Maryanne will let go of the coat and pick up her glass, but she doesn't. Instead, she takes a pair of gloves out of Will's pockets. She holds them in her hands for a moment, as if his hands are in them, then she puts them on. "I gave him these gloves for Christmas."

Cecilia widens her eyes at me. "They're beautiful, Maryanne."

"One hundred and fifty-nine dollars I paid for these gloves. I drove all the way to Boston for them. I kept imagining them on his hands, you know, year after year. How the leather would get worn across the knuckles. How he would wear them when he was shoveling snow or driving or—" And then all at once she stops herself and blurts out: "Can I ask you guys a personal question?"

Cecilia looks at me significantly. "Maryanne, really, I think we're sort of beyond the asking-permission stage. Fire away. Anything goes. Right, Beth?"

I murmur my assent. But the truth is, I'm not sure I want to hear what's coming. I can tell from Maryanne's face that, for her, the entire evening has been leading up to this point. This is the reason she's been sitting in someone's guest room, on a pile of coats, listening to us theorize Will; it's the reason she came to this party in the first place.

"Did Will ever—did he ever tell you he loved you?"

Cecilia and I flinch as if we've been slapped across the mouth. I look at her. She shakes her head. "No," she says. "I said it, like a goddamned fool, but he never said it back."

"He never said it to me," I say. "But I never said it to him, either. I almost did, once. At the time it seemed so obvious that we both felt that way. It seemed like it went without saying."

"It never goes without saying," Cecilia says.

"That's true."

"You know what he'd say instead?" Cecilia asks. "He'd say, I love your face, I love your ass, I love the way you laugh or walk or talk or whatever. But never, I love you."

"He did that with me, too. He parceled out his love in these safe little packages."

Maryanne is quiet, and we remember her question.

"Did he say it to you?" Cecilia whispers.

Maryanne nods, her eyes shiny again with tears. "The last time was on Christmas morning," she says, lifting her gloved hands.

"Christmas morning? That's low," Cecilia says. "He's slipping, don't you think, Beth? He's getting sloppy."

I nod, still feeling the stab in my chest from this newest bit of information.

"I'm sorry," Maryanne says. "It's just, he told me he hadn't said it in a long time. So that's why I asked you. To see if at least that part was true." She took off the gloves and put them back into Will's pockets.

"Keep them," Cecilia says.

"What?"

"Keep the gloves. Give them to some homeless person on the street. Burn them, if you want."

Maryanne looks at us, considering. "He'll know I took them. He'll figure it out."

"Nah. You know how he is. Absent-minded about his stuff, then frantic, turning his place upside down when he's lost something. I spent more Saturday afternoons than I care to count digging around his apartment, his car, everywhere, helping him find his stuff. He won't remember if he wore those gloves to the party, or left them in the car, or what. It'll drive him crazy. He'll be thinking about those gloves for weeks."

"But if he wore them here, then Julie will remember—"

"He didn't," I say, picturing the two of them arriving. "He was holding Julie's hand when they walked in. Neither of them had on gloves."

Maryanne finally agrees, folding the gloves carefully into her purse. I'm worried that instead of giving them to the Salvation Army, as she says she's going to do, she'll use them to build a Will-shrine in her apartment. But maybe that's okay for now. Maybe she needs some more time.

Cecilia looks at her watch. "I'm supposed to meet Mike down at the Main Event. He's playing in a dart tournament." She makes a face, but I know she likes Mike, a travel agent she's been dating, and enjoys these evenings in male-dominated bars where she can reign supreme. She finds her coat at the bottom of the pile. Maryanne takes hers, saying, "I'll walk out with you. I can't handle this party right now."

"You'll get used to it. After Julie comes someone else. If he ever gets married, I get to have the bachelorette party, and I'm inviting every single one of us. An all-nighter. Legendary."

"Can you imagine? That'd change the bride's mind," I say.

"No," Maryanne says. "She'd just think, look at all these women, and he chose me." We laugh and embrace, a big three-woman hug that goes on for a long time.

After Cecilia and Maryanne leave, I go into the living room. There's a party going on here: half-finished drinks and plates of food sitting on bookshelves and end tables; people I know, and some I don't, in intense, slightly drunken conversations; Irish folk music playing in the background. A guy with a beard who was recently hired in the sociology department (or is it political science?) is sitting on the floor, studying the CD selection. He looks sincere, and I make a mental note to ask Cecilia about him.

All this time, I have been hyper-aware of Will's position on the couch. That's still the first thing I do under these circumstances— scan the room for his location. Not because I want to see him, but because I don't. Right now he's sitting as close to Julie as possible. They look happy. That's the thing. They look so happy. And I remember that happiness, the way it felt to submerge myself into someone else. I've never lost myself in a man the way I did with Will, and I'm still not sure why it happened that way.

And now, as I make small talk with a man I know from work, I'm also remembering a Saturday afternoon, waiting for Will. He was coming over for dinner and I was restless, killing time until I could reasonably begin fixing him dinner, because every peeled shrimp and every minced clove of garlic brought me closer to the moment when he would knock on my door. It was all I wanted to do anymore—be with Will, or think about him, or wait for him, or talk to him on the phone. I remember standing at the kitchen sink, a half-peeled tiger shrimp in my hand, the table already set, my velvet dress laid out, eyebrows plucked, legs shaved, perfume applied, chocolate mousse chilling, wine breathing—and suddenly it occurred to me: Will was skiing. At that very moment, while I stood in the kitchen digging out shrimp dung with my newly manicured fingernails, *Will was skiing.*

For a long time I stood against the sink, trying not to hyperventilate, trying to think of how I used to fill my free time before I became Will's lover. But I couldn't recall that self, the self who had other friends, interesting hobbies, travel plans. Somewhere along the line I lost track of her.

So that night I made a decision. I decided to fly down to Florida for a week. Things were slow at work, and my boss would be thrilled if I used some vacation time. That night at dinner I told Will I was going, and would love it if he could join me. He demurred, as I knew he would; he had a story to write, a deadline, a new assignment. And I thought, fine. That's it then. The last invitation issued, and turned down.

I went to Key West. I lay out in the sun. I bought a big pink straw hat and a coffee mug with alligators on it. I visited the Hemingway house with all the six-toed cats and the palm trees in the front yard. In the mornings I swam a hundred laps in the hotel pool. In the evenings I ate hamburgers and drank Margaritas at an outdoor cafe. I went to bed early and read mysteries, and slept alone on crisp white sheets.

When I got back, Will and I had one last date. A week later I saw him walking across campus with Maryanne. And that, as they say, was that.

The party is winding down now. People start to leave. Outside it's snowing—I can see big fat flakes, purple in the streetlights—

and I want to escape into that pure cold air. I want to breathe it in and clear the alcohol haze, and I want to be in my own quiet house, alone. I find my coat and say my goodbyes. "Be careful walking home, Beth," someone calls out. "I will," I answer from the living room doorway, tying a scarf around my head. "You be careful too." I lift my eyes as I say this, and find myself looking straight at Julie without really meaning to. She looks so young and vulnerable sitting there, her face flushed and her pupils dilated, Will's attention washing over her like a wave, and I see her getting swept away, and before I think about what I'm doing I say it again, softly, right to her: "Be careful." She looks startled and pretends not to hear me, but she does hear me. She knows exactly what I am saying. Will touches her arm, and she turns to him. The expression on her face must have changed, because he goes further, he takes her hand, he clasps it in both of his. I move for the door, and then I am outside, walking fast in the cold snowy air and feeling a surge of energy, a thrill in my bones, a rise of laughter, an unchaining of my heart.

# how i spent my summer vacation

During Libby's eighteenth summer she thought of her body as separate from herself, and watched in amazement as it did things it had never done before. First she bought a uniform. The store was called Uniformly Great, and it was located in a strip mall next to a Japanese restaurant where later in the summer she would drink Navy Grogs and eat Sauteed Happy Family with her guitar teacher. The choices were limited: white slacks, white shoes, and a polyester smock in the same light blue as the gym shorts she'd worn to play those humiliating games of field hockey in junior high.

Now she was grown up; she had a job as a nurse's aide; she was housesitting for her parents; she was smoking cigarettes. Libby's parents once had money, but had poorly invested and otherwise mismanaged it, so Libby had to work. Her sister, Gwen, an actress in New York, remembered the flush times. She talked nostalgically about "those good old rich days" as if she were one of Libby's senile patients and not a twenty-four-year-old sharing an apartment in the Village with two other waiter-actors. Libby had always worked, ever since she was fourteen, though she had never worked this hard: lifting and wiping and feeding the bodies in her care. Her favorite was an old fat Irish woman named Mrs. O'Hara who always seemed mildly surprised when told she needed cleaning up. Though how she could avoid noticing the stench that rose from her adult diapers, Libby didn't know. Libby liked her anyway, because Mrs. O'Hara was so serene and grateful and dignified—she seemed above her own shit even as she sat in it. She purred with pleasure when Libby rubbed her back with lotion to prevent bedsores, thanked her in her thick Irish brogue as Libby fed her tapioca pudding, smiled and clucked and nodded while Libby read her stories from *Reader's Digest* about heroic rescues and near-death experiences. Maybe it was just her responsiveness that Libby loved about her. She was engaged in her life, even in its current reduced shitty state.

Libby was, otherwise, alone, at least at the beginning of the summer. In the beginning she went to work at seven every morning and at three-thirty came home, sunned herself, swam in the backyard pool, had a glass of wine, made herself dinner, read or watched TV, and was in bed by nine. Her parents were pursuing their summer projects. Her father was in San Francisco, researching a series of articles. Her mother was in Rhode Island, teaching sculpting for a college arts program. Libby knew at some level that a divorce was imminent. But she pushed the thought away, watered her mother's ferns and fuchsia that grew thickly in the sunroom, checked the chlorine levels of the pool, and thought vaguely about beginning college in the fall.

Was she looking forward to college? Not particularly. She had spent the last four years at boarding school, which was why she had no friends in town. The people she knew from school lived in the city or elsewhere, and at the moment they were on exotic trips with their parents (Scandinavia, New Zealand, Peru) or else spending the summer in the Hamptons or on the Cape. Libby had been something of a loner at school anyway. She hadn't dated much, especially in her last year. Her one boyfriend had been so shy he hardly kissed her. Instead, they spent long evenings holding hands in the back of the library, while their peers humped away in the woods or, the really brave ones, in the dormitories after lights out. Now, as she thought about being eighteen, as she thought about college, her virginity seemed a burden to her, something to shed like an old flaking skin. The summer, though only two weeks old, began to seem a terrible drudgery. She wondered how people got through their long awful minimum-wage lives. It was at this point she decided to take guitar lessons.

Libby had always wanted to learn to play the guitar. At school a beautiful girl named Lara used to sing mournful folk songs in the dormitory lounge until she sold her guitar for seven hundred hits of speed. Not long after that she went home to Long Island for the weekend and never came back. Libby fantasized about being the kind of girl who could play guitar and sing in front of people as if they weren't even there. She read the classifieds in the local paper and found an ad that read, simply, Guitar Lessons, Good Rates, Call Brad. She found her father's old guitar (because of course he had one) in the guest room closet and thought, Maybe Brad will be cute.

When her mother next called to check in, Libby told her about the Danskin leotards she had found on sale that week, but not about the guitar lessons. She told her about Mrs. O'Hara, but not about the cigarettes. She exhaled smoke quietly as they spoke. "Oh, and we need to get the front door lock fixed," she said. "It isn't working. You lock it but then if you just pull the door hard, it opens."

"Call a locksmith, honey, and have them replace it. Look in the Yellow Pages."

"Okay," Libby said. But she didn't, because during the day she didn't think about it, and when she locked up the house at night, she brought the dog, Dear Prudence, into her bedroom. She reminded herself that they lived in a safe neighborhood where nothing ever happened, which was mostly true.

ON THE DAY OF HER FIRST LESSON, she spent the early afternoon getting ready. At four o'clock she arrived at Brad's parents' house, or rather, mobile home. She had never been to a mobile home park before. Each home was fully landscaped, with a miniature picket fence and trellises and shrubbery, and most of them even had attached carports and concrete front stoops. Libby knocked tentatively on the storm door, looking back at her car, where Dear Prudence sat panting and sniffing out the window.

Brad was not whom she had pictured while giving herself an apricot facial. He was older, for one thing. He told her he was twenty-seven, separated from his wife, and only staying with his parents temporarily. "I'm on disability. Back injury. I work in a box factory."

"A box factory?" Libby didn't know what else to say. They were standing in the living room, where the floral-patterned furniture looked brand new. The matching curtains were pulled tight against the brilliant summer day. A large ashtray with a mermaid painted on the bottom of it sat in the middle of a glass coffee table.

"Yeah. We make boxes." When Brad smiled she noticed a silver tooth and a spark in his eyes that she liked. She also noticed a tiny chip of a diamond in one earlobe. She took an inventory of the other things about him as he talked about his job as foreman, and the troubles he had with his crew. His brown hair brushed his collar. Just long enough, she thought. She hated really long hair on men. Beard, large green eyes. He was too skinny though. Skinny, hunched shoulders. Hollow cheeks. And his forehead was too big. With his hair combed straight back, his brow bulged. And he worked in a box factory. And he lived with his parents, even though he was almost thirty. And they lived in a *trailer*.

"Oh," Libby said, blushing, realizing he had just asked her something—something about what she did. "Right now I'm working as a nurse's aide." She felt funny about saying she was going to college in the fall.

"Now that's tough work. Old people?"

"Yeah."

"I play jazz guitar," he explained, taking her guitar out of its case, motioning for her to sit on the stiff couch.

She remembered the story of a girl in her class visiting her boyfriend's parents in their Park Avenue apartment; she was sitting on a white couch when she gradually became aware that her period had started, and she was bleeding all over the expensive leather. Libby flushed again, but Brad didn't notice. He was tuning her guitar and talking about his band. "There's just three of us, actually. The percussionist is a fuck-up."

She waited to see whether Brad was going to apologize for swearing in front of her, and felt relieved when he didn't. She slouched a little, feeling comfortable, and was glad for the tan on her legs.

"We're trying to get a break. This guy I play with, Kevin? He has a connection in the city. You don't happen to sing, do you? We need a good vocalist."

"No." Libby smiled, imagining herself in a smoky Village bar—the one she had gone to with her sister when she turned eighteen and legal—wearing a slinky black spaghetti-strap dress. She saw herself under a single spotlight, singing into a microphone, eyes closed, while Brad stood behind her, nodding and strumming and smiling in his sleepy way.

"Okay, here." He handed her the guitar.

Libby felt silly, as if she had just been handed a huge inflatable hot dog. "I don't know how to read music or anything."

Brad shrugged. "That's cool. I'll teach you." He picked up his own guitar, which had been leaning casually against the loveseat, played a quick riff—by way of showing off, Libby thought, or maybe he couldn't help himself—and began to show her some chords.

"My fingers don't go that way," she said.

"They will. You need to practice."

He put his guitar down and sat next to her on the couch, moving her fingers to form a G-chord. His lips were very red, and Libby decided he was probably smart to have a beard, to distract from the redness of his lips and to fill out his gaunt cheeks.

Brad wrote out some chord progressions for her on a piece of music paper. She gave him the dollar bills she had folded up in her pocket before leaving home. He nodded his thanks and lit up a Salem. "I'll walk you out," he said. He opened the door for her and she stepped into the bright afternoon, clumsily bumping the guitar case against her legs.

Dear Prudence, ever alert, frowned at the sight of Brad, then began her deep growl that was prefatory to a bark.

"Hush, Prudie," Libby commanded, and the dog ducked her head and wagged her tail.

"Does she like the water? The lake's just down there." He indicated the direction with his chin.

It was the same lake where Libby used to water-ski in junior high, the summer before boarding school. "She loves it. We have a pool at home, I mean my parents do—" but she was sorry she had mentioned the pool. You had to be careful about things like that; people sometimes thought you were a snob. But Brad didn't seem to care.

"I never learned to swim," he said.

"This close to the lake?"

"Oh, I didn't grow up here. The mobile home is new." He emphasized "mobile home," disdain in his voice. "If you want, we can take your dog down to the beach. It's just a short walk."

"Sure," Libby said, letting Prudence out and grabbing her cigarettes from the dashboard. The dog made a show of sniffing Brad, then ran off schizophrenically down the path ahead of them, sensing unchlorinated water in the air.

"My mother was always weird about pools," Brad said. He lit Libby's cigarette, cupping his hand around hers even though there was no wind. "She had a sister who got polio from a neighborhood pool, you know, back when polio was a big deal. It didn't matter to her that I'd been vaccinated or anything." Libby remembered the little Dixie cups full of clear tasteless liquid. "She never encouraged me to swim and I don't know, I just was never that interested. I was always inside, listening to music."

Libby nodded. They reached a small beach, and she threw a stick for Prudence and laughed as she bounded into the water, then couldn't find it, her head jerking around like a cartoon dog whose dog dish has just been swiped.

"I love swimming. It's like—being somewhere else."

"Ah, yes. Self-transcendence. You're talking to an old pro on that score."

"I was on the swim team for four years. Sometimes I feel like I've spent more time in the water than out."

"An athlete, huh? So what's with the smoking?"

Libby shrugged. She had taken on something new, allowed some new part of herself to emerge. "It's just temporary."

"So you're what—nineteen? Twenty?"

"Eighteen."

"College in September?"

"Mmm hmm. Looks that way, anyway." Libby put out her cigarette and whistled for Prudence, who was snapping at the water. They walked back to the mobile home park, and Brad got her a towel for the dog, a large pink "S" monogrammed in the middle of it. "Put it on the seat. You can bring it back next week."

She thanked him and got into her car and he smiled, the silver tooth shining in the sun, hands in his jeans pockets, while Prudence panted and trembled with happiness, as if to say, What a day this turned out to be, after all.

WORK, THAT WEEK, SEEMED HARDER. Mrs. O'Hara wasn't doing well. One day she didn't talk to Libby at all. Then she seemed to perk up again. The R.N. on duty shook her head. "That's the way it is with these folks. Up and down, then finally, down." At home Libby washed out her uniform every night, watered the plants, swam. She practiced her guitar, forcing her fingers to go the ways that Brad had showed her, like cramped arthritic claws. "I'm learning to play the guitar," she said as she gave Mrs. O'Hara her sponge bath. But Mrs. O'Hara didn't respond. "Maybe I'll come play you a song one day." Libby turned the crank on the bed, opened the curtains all the way, arranged Mrs. O'Hara's bed jacket, put her favorite Lawrence Welk tape on her player. "Okay, then, Mrs. O'Hara," Libby said. "I'll be back at lunch." But Mrs. O'Hara just stared blandly at the wall.

When Libby's mother called from Rhode Island and said, "Are you getting lonely, honey?" Libby choked up. She hadn't realized she was lonely until this minute. She got off the phone so her mother wouldn't know she had begun to cry. She walked from empty room to room, hugging herself. She buried her face in Dear Prudence's fur, lay on each bed in the house, drank a glass of wine, felt worse. She had no friends. She was alone in this house. Where was everybody? Why had they left her alone here? All that talk about Libby being so mature, so capable of staying on her own, wasn't true. Soon she'd have to leave home again. She didn't want to go to college. She didn't want to stay home. She didn't want to practice guitar or join any more swim teams or watch TV or make herself dinner or smoke a cigarette or not smoke a cigarette. Finally she put a leash on Dear Prudence and went for a long walk. Prudence loved it, and after a while it was the dog who made Libby better, with her tongue lolling, her laughing black gums, her fast little legs like a mechanical toy, her brown adoring eyes and her large doggy heart.

After each lesson with Brad, Libby stayed a little longer. Once they went out for pizza. Another time she gave him a ride to his friend Kevin's, since Brad didn't have a car and had to hitchhike everywhere. Brad and Kevin invited her to stay. Libby was flattered. She drank a beer and smoked cigarettes while Brad and Kevin jammed in the living room. She felt like someone else, someone older and prettier and cooler. The music was good, as far as she could tell, and she watched Brad with new admiration. When she left Kevin's house, Brad walked her to the door and kissed her on the cheek, and whispered, "Can I see you before next week?" Libby smiled and nodded, and on the way home she drove with the windows down and the radio on loud—Heart's "Magic Man" was playing—and felt excited and happy for the first time all summer.

Brad called the next day. She went to his house. His parents were home. They looked old, with small pinched faces, like Libby's grandparents. Brad took her to his room, a small room with a twin bed and a lot of stereo equipment. He rolled a joint and asked if she wanted to get stoned. She said okay, though she had never much liked the disconnected way pot made her feel. In the living room his parents were watching a game show. Brad lit the joint and held the smoke, then passed the joint to her. The game show host's voice went up and down. Brad put on some music. "It's so weird living here," he said.

Libby nodded. She didn't trust herself to speak. Brad went to the kitchen and brought back two beers. She was so thirsty. Summer-thirsty: hot afternoons playing badminton with her father, or lying on inflatable rafts in the pool with Gwen, trying to knock each other over.

"You're smiling," Brad said, after what seemed like a long time.

"I'm stoned." She smiled back. "I was thinking about summer. How they'd always make you write, 'How I Spent My Summer Vacation.'"

"Yeah. Why couldn't they think of something interesting for once."

"You always felt like you had to come up with something really cool. Not what actually happened, how bored you were or the rotten family vacations where it rained the whole time and everyone got on each other's nerves."

"Right. How about: 'How I Really Spent My Summer Vacation.' My dad lost his job and drank too much. I beat off eight times a day."

Libby blushed, lit a cigarette. "I lit firecrackers in the woods with the neighborhood kids and almost burned down a dozen trees."

"I lost my virginity to Sallie Wilkinson in her garage and we never spoke to each other again after that."

Libby shook her head.

"So who'd you lose it to?"

She shook her head again.

"Sorry—wow. That was none of my goddamned business. You want to smoke another joint?"

"Better not. I've got to drive home."

"Don't go yet. Don't leave me with … them …" He pantomimed Igor and indicated his parents on the other side of the wall.

"Okay." She giggled.

"So, give me a prediction. What's this year's essay going to say?"

"How I spent my summer vacation?"

"Yeah."

Libby shook her head. "I worked cleaning up shit off of old people for minimum wage. I fed them baby food. I talked to the ones who could still talk. I watered my mother's African violets and her Boston ferns and talked to my parents on the phone and acted like everything was fine." She leaned over and kissed Brad quickly on the mouth. "I kissed my guitar teacher."

"Just once?"

She leaned over and kissed him again, longer this time.

"Just twice?"

She smiled. "I kissed my guitar teacher many times, and then one night when no parents were around, I lost my virginity to him."

"Wow."

"Sorry. I shouldn't have said that. I'm fucked up." She started to stand. He pulled her gently back on the twin bed. The bedspread was that ribbed kind, brown; they had an old one at home that Prudence slept on.

"No. I'm glad you said it. I'm completely flattered."

"I feel like a total jerk."

"Just slow down. Nothing has to happen."

"I want it to happen. Do you think I'm a slut?" she asked solemnly.

"Given the virginity factor, no—" and they both giggled, then giggled uncontrollably, and couldn't stop. She liked him then.

"Can we just forget what I said?"

"Yes. No, but yes." He kissed her. "No, on second thought. Definitely no."

"No, what?"

"I don't remember." And they giggled again.

"I don't want it to be this big deal, okay? Don't talk about the fact that it's my first time. Just act like it's our first time."

"That should be easy."

"Okay. Don't talk about it anymore. And don't get mad if I change my mind because I'm really messed up now."

"Okay."

But she didn't change her mind. They ordered a pizza, and Brad's parents went to play bridge at a friend's house in a neighboring town. After the pizza they drank more beer, and after the beer they took off just their shirts and lay together on his bed just kissing until that was too much, and so they kept going, and going, until they had done everything and it was late and Libby felt okay but really just wanted to be alone. So she left, just as Brad's parents were returning. They waved at her from their car, their small white hands like moths at the windshield. She waved back. Driving home she didn't feel any different. She played the radio loud and opened all the windows but didn't sing along. Brad was nice. He had been sweet about everything. Gentle. Serious. She sat in her car in the driveway for a few minutes before going inside. The phone was ringing.

"Hi. I just wanted to be sure you got home okay."

"I did, thanks."

"You all right?"

"I'm fine. Just tired."

"No regrets?"

"Of course not. I had fun."

"Can I call you tomorrow?"

"Sure. But I have to go to work. So call after four."

"Okay. Sleep well."

"Okay."

"And Libby?"

"Yeah?"

"Thank you."

"For what?"

"Just, thank you."

Libby frowned. This irritated her. "Sure. You're welcome. Good night." She hung up. Dear Prudence was dancing around the kitchen. She hadn't been fed. "Sorry, old girl. Sorry I'm so late." She fed the dog. Let her out, let her in. Pulled the door shut. Locked it. Even though the lock didn't work. She pretended it did.


LIBBY WENT TO PLANNED PARENTHOOD and got a prescription for the Pill. She kept the plastic wheel in her purse, next to her cigarettes. This was her life now, and she watched it unfold: waking up at six, usually with Brad next to her in her too-small double bed. Then breakfast and a shower and putting on the polyester uniform and driving Brad to the highway on her way to work—he hitched home from there. By ten, she was sweating with the effort of sponge baths, dressing old limbs, cleaning up messes. She listened to herself talking to the other aides, dropping her *g*'s to sound more like them, feigning indifference about the work she was doing. She was becoming detached from herself. She was ten degrees off, or twenty, a ghostly image of herself watching her body doing these things—with the patients, with the other aides, with Brad. It was confusing, like being stoned: she felt somehow that she wasn't her true self, but she also didn't know who that true self was. By three o'clock she was off work, and most days she drove out to Brad's parents' to pick him up. She showered again, changed clothes, had a beer with Brad, sometimes a joint, then there was dinner at her house or at the Japanese restaurant in the same strip mall as Uniformly Great, where she had gone just two days after graduation to buy her uniform. Libby had a collection of tiny paper parasols from the Navy Grogs they drank there, blue and yellow and pink and green, the happy bright colors of party streamers. She looked at the parasols, sitting in a coffee mug on her dresser that her mother had given her ("You are the music of my life," with a dog playing a fiddle) while Brad did things to her in her bed. In the beginning she was embarrassed. She was self-conscious. But he talked to her in his low raspy jazz-musician voice and he touched her and felt her and moved inside her in ways she had never anticipated someone doing. She kept her eyes closed the whole time, always, so that it felt to her like her own private ride and not anything really to do with Brad. Because if she thought too much about the Brad element, or if she listened too closely to the noises he made—noises that frightened her, or made her want to laugh—then the ride was over. Part of her wished they'd never begun.

Afterward, she always went swimming. She liked swimming naked, in the dark. It made her feel as if she were in a movie. Brad sat on a lawn chair, messing around on his guitar or smoking a joint, talking about how his parents pissed him off or about how he was being screwed. His agent was screwing him. So was the record company that had offered him a contract last year. Everything was unfair. Things kept falling through. He didn't know why. No one would return his calls.

Libby floated around, half-listening, kicking her feet desultorily through the water that always looked thick to her in the dark, the moonlight chopped up and scattered across its surface like torn luminescent paper. "You should learn to swim," she said to him once, as she did a perfect sidestroke up and down the length of the pool.

"I should do a lot of things," he said. Libby couldn't argue with that one.

ONE DAY LIBBY RECEIVED A LETTER FROM ALLISON, the roommate her college had matched her up with. "Dear Libby, Hi! I'm your future roommate!" the letter began. "Here's a little bit about me: I'm planning on being a math major, but I might go the economics route instead. My hobbies include running cross country, playing clarinet (since second grade!!) and math club (president for two years!!). I have two brothers and two sisters, all younger than me. I have a stereo to bring to school—I've seen our room and it's pretty small so let me know what you want to bring. Your roomie, Allison."

"She sounds like a dweeb," Brad said.

Libby shrugged. They were eating at the Japanese restaurant. She folded the letter and put it back in her purse. Dear Allison, she thought. I have no idea about my major or anything else. My hobbies did include learning guitar until I started sleeping with my teacher. Paying him seemed sort of weird, so I quit. I have a sister I never see, ditto with my parents. I'll do my best to quit smoking since I myself requested a nonsmoking roommate and I'm pretty sure you are one. Your pal, Libby.

"I thought you didn't want to go to college," Brad said, finishing his second drink.

Libby frowned. Had she actually said that? She twirled a yellow parasol between her thumb and index finger. It was almost the end of July. Her thighs stuck to the vinyl seat of their favorite booth. She unstuck them and lit a cigarette.

"A bad thing happened at work today," she said, exhaling. "Mrs. O'Hara died."

"About time."

"That's not very nice, Brad."

"Sorry. How'd she die?"

"Just—died. Heart stopped, I guess. I went in to feed her some tapioca and she wouldn't wake up." Libby was speaking in her new casual way but the truth was Mrs. O'Hara's death had shaken her. She could still see her: a little greyer than usual, the greasy hair falling in limp strands—she was supposed to have her hair washed and set that afternoon. Libby had stood, the bowl of pudding in her hand, watching the large chest that did not rise and fall.

"She had stopped talking, hadn't she?"

"Yeah."

"Her number was up. She's probably relieved as hell to be out of that mess."

"Yeah, she probably is." Their dinner arrived. Libby picked up her chopsticks. Outside, the lady from the uniform store was locking up. Libby remembered how short she was, her dyed black hair and magenta lipstick. She watched her get into her car, wondered where she lived, what her life was like. Had she always wanted a uniform store? Had she once been a person in uniform? A nurse, maybe, or a factory worker?

"I've been thinking," Brad began, "maybe I should move up to Vermont with you. We could rent an apartment together. I could get some gigs at the bars there. It's a cool town. I've driven through it before."

When you had a car, Libby thought, except she was too taken aback by the other part to fully think it.

"What about Allison?" This was a stupid thing to say, she knew, but it was the only thing she could think of besides: no, never, not on your life.

"Who?"

"My roommate. I mean, my parents have already paid a deposit on my room and meal plan and everything."

"You can get out of all that. If you want to."

"Actually, I can't." She just remembered. "Freshmen have to live in the dorms. There's a residency requirement the first year."

Brad arranged food on his plate in his meticulous way. Spreading out a bed of rice. Spooning the shrimp carefully over one side, the vegetables on the other. "Aren't you going to eat?" Libby nodded. A drop of perspiration trickled down her back. She served herself a spoonful of vegetables. "So you have to live in the dorm."

"Right," she said, not looking at him. On the other side of the restaurant, a family of four sat together. The parents were talking. A girl about Libby's age, maybe a year younger, looked around as if bored. How stupid, Libby thought. I'd change places with you in a minute.

"I could still move up there." He put a shrimp neatly in his small mouth, the red lips wet, the skinny shoulders hunched over his plate.

Where were the words? Why was this so hard—just to open her mouth and say, No? No, that is not a good idea?

Brad smiled in that half-smile way that hid the silver tooth. She had once found it impish; now it looked snide. "Okay. You're not going to talk. But obviously you have an opinion. You want to go off to college and leave all this behind. This summer—what?— fling."

"Brad—"

"No. I see how it is. Find a guitar teacher. He'd probably be cool. Get—experienced. A past, to tell your college friends about."

"It wasn't like that," Libby said. She wasn't sure if it was or not.

"Sure. It wasn't like that."

Libby watched the sullen girl at the other table stand up and slouch and scuff her way to the restroom, her flip-flops slapping against the floor, her fingers tugging at her halter top. How was it that Allison had already seen their dorm room? How was it that Mrs. O'Hara just—died? How was it that Libby, who had so often wished for a boyfriend in the last year, ended up with this boyfriend?

They finished their meal in silence. Libby paid the bill in cash; Brad's disability had run out, and he hadn't gone back to work yet. "I'm not feeling very well," she said as she drove him home. "I'm sorry. I'm upset about Mrs. O'Hara. I'll call you tomorrow, okay?"

But Brad didn't answer her. He slammed the car door shut and walked away, his fists in his jeans pockets. Libby started to call after him. Then a new possibility occurred to her that went like this: So what? So what if Brad is angry? Brad is mad, she sang to herself. Mad Brad. Who cares? Nobody cares. I don't care. She pulled her car out of the driveway and turned on the radio. Fleetwood Mac was playing. She loved Fleetwood Mac. She never could have listened to them if Brad had been in the car. Too pop rock for him. She turned it up. "You can go your own way!" she yelled. "You can call it another lonely day!" On the way home she stopped at an import shop and bought candles and a brightly patterned Indian bedspread and a wicker trash basket and two cushions with tiny mirrors and sequins sewn on them. She bought a greeting card with a watercolor of two girls on the front, walking through a garden. It was blank inside. Dear Allison, she thought as the clerk rang up her purchases, I can't wait to meet you. I've had a busy summer, working mostly. I'll be glad to start school. A fresh start. Do you know what I mean? Your future friend, Libby.

She felt so much better she stopped at Howland's and bought two sweaters and a pair of jeans. She threw away the cigarettes in her purse. When she pulled into her driveway, she saw Prudence standing in the front yard, wagging her tail slowly, as if not sure whom to expect. She ran up to Libby. "Oh, girl, did I leave you outside all day? I'm sorry, old thing." But when Libby went inside and smelled the cigarette smoke, she remembered, again, the broken lock.

"Brad?" she called.

"In here." He was sitting in the sunroom. She turned on the lights. His reflection appeared in the sliding glass doors that led out to the pool.

"Hi," she said, trying to sound nonchalant. "How'd you get here?"

"I just came to say I'm sorry. I didn't mean to act like such a jerk." He glanced at the packages she was carrying. "Glad to see you're feeling better."

"How'd you get here?"

"Hitched, naturally. Got lucky. Some guy in a VW bug brought me all the way to the end of your street."

"Look, Brad—"

"I just came to talk to you for a minute, to say what I should have said before. Please just listen, Libby. I know I'm no prize right now. I don't even have a fucking car. I can't even afford to divorce my bitch wife. But it's just a bad patch. And I'm in love with you, Libby. I should've told you this weeks ago. I don't want to lose you."

Libby put down her bags. She sat on the couch next to Brad. Her heart was pounding. Even though he was saying these things, something else was happening. She wasn't sure what. "Brad, I'm sorry. I care about you a lot." Under his beard she could see a smirk, but she kept going. "But I'm eighteen. I'm going to college. I'm not ready—to live with anyone right now."

"Except Allison." He smiled.

"Right. Except Allison."

"All right. I'm glad at least we're clear about that." He put out his cigarette, leaned over and kissed her. He touched her face. She didn't want to kiss him. But she thought, Okay, this will be the last time. He pulled her closer to him, moaned. She thought, I was doing this with him last night, and the night before. What's wrong with one more time? He pulled off her shirt, kissed her breasts. She didn't want him to do that, or the next thing, but she kept talking herself through it, thinking, it's the last time, and besides I'm not so sure what would happen if I said no. I'm not sure that would work. Let's just get him out of here with his dignity. It's just sex. Just her body. In the dark glass of the sliding doors she could see her pale ghost self, lying on the couch, could see Brad above her, unbuckling his jeans, could see him—through the plants she had watered and forgotten to water—push himself into her. She closed her eyes as she always did, only this time she was not riding any wave, and this time he did not want her to close her eyes.

"Look at me, Libby," he said through clenched teeth.

She opened her eyes. What she saw frightened her. Had he always looked like this in the middle of sex? She tried to turn her head, to watch their reflections, to see herself as over there, not here, not on her parents' couch doing this thing that she didn't want to do: this thing felt like a drilling or a pounding or a stabbing into the body that wasn't separate after all but was hers. Was her. Brad kept his hand on her face, holding her chin and jaws so that he was almost hurting her. What would happen if his hand slipped down to her throat? She needed to focus. She needed to stay calm. It was just Brad. Her boyfriend. Her lover. Nothing would happen.

He moved his hand off her face and shuddered over her. He lay on top of her, and she wondered if he had fallen asleep. Then he rolled over, and she began, slowly, to slip off the edge of the couch.

"Stay with me for a while," he whispered.

"I'm just going for a swim," she whispered back. She forced herself to kiss the red lips, quickly, the way she had done that first time. "I'll be right back." He started to grab her arm but she was already at the door, sliding it open, and running across the cool grass. He can't swim, she kept thinking. He can't swim! It almost made her laugh, except that he was running after her, yelling her name like a curse. She flipped open the latch on the pool gate and dove into the water. When she came up for air, he was standing, panting, at the side of the pool.

"Get out of the water, Libby."

"Why are you doing this?" A sob caught in her throat. She was shaking. "Just go home, Brad. Just leave me alone." She watched him, the big forehead, the arms hanging by his sides, useless but tense.

"All summer you've been pulling this shit. Sometimes I think we're a couple. Other times I feel like you're just passing the time. I just want you to spend five minutes with me. Really with me. Just five minutes. You owe me that much."

She owed him that much? The air felt cool on her wet face. She could almost smell the end of summer, dying leaves, the apple trees in the backyard, and the maples. She had climbed those trees, made secret places with old baby blankets and books and stuffed animals, places for waiting and watching. Her mother would call her—*Libby, Libby honey, time for dinner*—and she would sit for a long time before climbing down, listening to the syllables tumbling toward her, the sounds of someone wanting her back, then the memory of the sounds.

Brad began pacing now, striding up and down the cement walk. She concentrated on her own arms and legs, moving them as slowly as possible in the water. Of course she was being unreasonable. She was freaking out over nothing. Wasn't she? She watched Brad, and went over what she knew: The car keys are on the table. My clothes are on the floor by the couch. He'll need a cigarette sometime in the next twenty minutes. The neighbors' lights were on when I got home.

She gauged how quickly she might have to move. Imagined herself doing the necessary things. Floated on her back, moon on her face, and waited.

# the two husbands

They had been drifting for an hour. There was no wind. Bill trimmed the mainsheet. But it didn't matter what he did with the mainsheet. They were dead in the water.

The sun had set but light still filled the sky. A sticky film from the humid lake air clung to their skins; a slightly chemical smell rose off the water. Katy sat on the bow, her feet dangling over the edge of the boat. Her mouth was dry from smoking a joint with Tree. She wasn't stoned anymore, just tired of sitting on the boat listening to the two men talk. She felt the waste of the day behind her, like the litter of beer cans in the galley. Her head ached.

"You could start the engine," Katy said. "We could motor in this time."

"You said that before. What's the hurry?" Bill was drunk. Bill never sounded drunk unless he was completely blottoed, but Katy could tell; there were other signs. Over the course of the afternoon he had consumed eleven beers. Katy always counted. It was a habit of hers. She also counted the out-of-state license plates whenever they made the Springfield trip. She counted the number of highway patrolmen they passed. She gambled, made deals in her head: If I get to an even number by the time we hit St. Jo, then everything will go fine. She kept track of Bill's beers as a way of keeping score, though later she would restrain herself from mentioning the number to him. She knew it wouldn't help.

Katy stood up. Probably the real reason they didn't motor in was that Bill had forgotten to bring gas. He'd never say so unless she asked directly, but she wouldn't ask. She looked at the water, eyes slowly traveling the distance between here and the marina.

"I bet I could swim and beat you in, the rate you're going," Katy said.

"I'd like to see you get in that water," Tree said, grinning.

Katy used to be married to Tree. His real name was Martin, but everyone called him Tree because of his size. Tree was drunk, too. Katy could tell right away with Tree, though. As soon as he cracked his second beer he started to slur his words. That was what got him into trouble. Katy looked at the men sitting in the stern, one resting his hand on the useless tiller and the other holding a can of Budweiser and thought, I am on a boat with two drunk husbands. She looked beyond the stern to the lake, a stretch of brown behind them. They hadn't seen any other boats out today. Nobody else had the day off like they did. In their line of business, you took time off when you felt like it. She looked down at the water again. The light in the sky was reflected in the water in pale dappled patterns. There was hardly a ripple on the surface. She imagined herself slipping into it like a cool bath, dunking her aching head, feeling the water cover her heavy hair. She was sure she could swim from here. She eyed the marina again. Maybe she was still a little stoned.

"How far do you think it is?" she asked the husbands.

"Quarter of a mile," Tree said. "Maybe less."

"Hell, it's farther than that," Bill said. "It's farther than it looks." He lit a cigarette and tossed the match into the water.

Bill knew distances better than Tree. Bill was smart that way. He could find his way around a strange city just by glancing at a map for a few minutes. He'd unfold it, study it, fold it up again, and that would be it. Tourists stopped to ask him directions and he could tell them exactly how to get to any museum, subway stop, national monument. Katy, who sometimes got lost in her own hometown, admired his innate sense of direction. Tree was nothing like Bill in that department. When Katy was married to Tree, they were always getting lost. They were hopeless in a strange place together. Once they drove around Chicago for three hours trying to find their way back to their hotel. Bill never got lost. Bill understood his physical relationship to the world. He thought in spatial, concrete terms—distances, weights, measures, angles. He read books on chaos and superforce and other theories of physics that Katy couldn't grasp. He had this mystical side. That's why she started sleeping with him. Tree was away, in detox, and Bill was living with them at the time. One night they stayed up late and he told her about gravity and electromagnetic fields, and they ended up in bed. It was wrong, she knew, to sleep with her husband's best friend. It was one of those bad things that sometimes happened. She blamed it on the coke, the bottle of Stoli Bill pulled from the freezer, but she knew it was really about her and Bill wanting to sleep together.

The strange thing was, when Tree got out of the hospital he didn't seem to mind the new arrangement all that much. "I'm sleeping downstairs with Bill now," she said when he walked in the door. He looked at her for a second, took a beer from the fridge, and said, "Okay. If that's what you want. I'm not going to stop you."

She didn't know what she wanted. But she knew she didn't want to sleep with an alcoholic anymore—someone who could spend a week throwing up, another three weeks in therapy, and then walk in the door and grab a beer as if it were a can of orange soda or something. After a few months of the new arrangement the three of them went to Vegas. Tree and Katy got a divorce. Bill and Katy got married. They referred to it as "that wild time." That wild time they went to Vegas and got married. It was an excuse for a party. Plus they did a little business. "Hey, it's tax-deductible," Tree joked.

Bill drank, too, but when Katy married him, she didn't think he had a problem. It didn't look like a problem. She wasn't sure now. His absolute cool, his control of every situation, his ease in strange places—maybe it was all a front. Katy looked at the shore, saw the corner of an A-frame house where somebody lived a quiet life. A family, maybe, or an old married couple. None of their friends understood how the three of them could stay in business together. But really, it wasn't that hard.

They inched forward. From here Katy could see the other boats tied to their moorings, their naked masts skeletons against the darkening sky. She pulled off her shirt. Underneath she was wearing a bright orange bikini. One of the husbands whistled. She couldn't tell which. They were both watching her. They were waiting to see if she would do it. She might have to do it just to prove to them she could. The trees on the shore were becoming indistinct, a blur of dark green. A breeze rose off the lake. It was the end of summer, the days were shorter, and a chill filled the evening air. Pretty soon sailing season would be over. In a month, two if they put it off, they would take the boat out of the water. They'd store it for the winter at Charlie's. Charlie was the one who had given them the boat. He had owed them money but they took the boat instead.

In the winter they would spend afternoons playing pool or watching videos or, if they'd been up all night, sleeping. Katy imagined the three of them old—forty, say—and still doing this. It was not what she would have predicted for herself as a life. She tried to remember what she had predicted. Teaching first grade? Or maybe running a little business, a clothing store. Katy's

Boutique. She crossed her arms against the chill, watched the water. Goose bumps rose on her bare skin like braille. She ran her fingers over the bumps. The closer the boat got to shore, the less reasonable it seemed to swim. Still, Katy thought. The feeling of her body in the water, buoyant, weightless. The sound of her breath. Her arms and legs propelling her forward, moving her gradually toward the dock and their car, and the bag of potato chips in the backseat. The boat behind her, growing smaller. The husbands, watching her go. It would be something.

# fits and starts

After my father left, I saw a lot more of him. He moved into an apartment in the city and I was invited to spend weekends there. I was ten years old and it was never made clear to me why he didn't live with us anymore. The speech he gave me and my mother the night he left was vague and difficult for me to follow, and she seemed to understand things in it that I did not, because she cried a lot while all I felt was sadness for her.

We lived in a large white house in Connecticut, a house my father had bought with radio money. That was what we called it, because my father had earned it doing radio voice-overs. After we moved to Connecticut, he started doing television commercials, and made even more money. But the days of the radio money were better days for us, because, my mother said, we were a real family then. I wasn't sure I remembered that time, but I took her word for it, and didn't ask any questions. There were certain things my mother and I never discussed. There was a side of life you just didn't talk about. I learned to turn my head, to pretend everything was all right. I imagined a small dark room like a linen closet where you stored things like divorce, sex, death, and I shut the door.

My mother used to sit at the dining room table with me while I ate breakfast. She wore a soft pink robe and drank coffee. In those days she had long brown hair that she wore in a French twist, but at breakfast her hair hung loose on her shoulders, and she twirled strands of it between her fingers while she talked to me about school or my friends or what she would fix us for dinner. After breakfast she brushed and fixed my hair, letting me choose the ribbon. She checked my tights for runs, and my shoes for scuff marks, then kissed me goodbye.

The school bus stop was across the street from our house. I could see our kitchen window from where I stood, and though I could not see her, I knew my mother was there: when the bus arrived, the kitchen curtains moved across the window like white flags, and I waved back.

After my father left, she stopped getting up with me. At first she said she wasn't feeling well. Then she didn't say anything. It was simply understood between us that she stayed in bed. When I came downstairs for breakfast, however, there was always a place set for me at the table. Everything was carefully laid out—place mat, cereal bowl, napkin, spoon. The cereal boxes were lined up at one end of the table, the sugar bowl placed at the other end. This symmetry was comforting, as if my world were in perfect balance. I sat at my place and looked at the designs in the blue and white wallpaper, making out faces and trees in the abstract swirls. Sometimes I moved to my mother's or father's seat for a change of scenery. But my place had the best view.

After a few weeks I learned to make my mother's coffee. It was the only way I could think of to get her out of bed without talking about it. Before leaving for school I tiptoed into her room. I loved the way she smelled—warm and soft, the smell of clean sheets and the lotions she used on her face and hands.

I knew she was awake. The shades were pulled and the room was dark, but I could see her fingers, twirling her hair against the pillow. "Bye Mom," I whispered.

"Bye honey," she whispered back, as if there were someone else in the room we were trying not to waken. "Have a good day at school."

"I will. You have a good day, too. I made your coffee," I whispered. "It should be done perking in just a few minutes."

"Thanks, baby," she said, squeezing my hand. I shut the door quietly behind me, and went into my room to brush my hair. I listened for signs of life. At the bus stop, I watched the kitchen window. Now, more often than not, the curtains waved over the glass and I waved back, relieved. On the days when the curtains did not move, I felt a sinking in my stomach, as if I had failed her. All day I looked at the clock, wondering, at each hour, Is she up yet? I thought about the coffee becoming thick and burnt-tasting in the percolator. I knew she wouldn't drink it that way. My mother liked her coffee fresh.

MY FATHER WAS DOING LAUNDRY DETERGENT COMMERCIALS. He walked into a woman's sunny laundry room, threw a cup of black viscous liquid onto a white shirt, and smiled when the woman gasped. "Don't you worry, Mrs. Jones, I have just the thing to take care of that," he said, pulling out a large container of liquid detergent from nowhere and pouring a capful of blue over the black stain.

"Why would a person do such a thing?" my mother said softly, genuinely perplexed. We watched the ugly stain disappear magically.

One night I dreamed of my father's apartment. It was big and empty; he hadn't had time to buy much furniture yet. In my dream, a woman dressed in a Spanish costume was doing a dance in the middle of the living room. She had castanets and a large, red, laughing mouth. When I woke up, I understood why my father left. But this wasn't something you talked about, even in your dreams, even to yourself. When I snooped in his medicine cabinet and found the bottle of nail polish remover, the box of tampons, the lipstick (bright red, just as I had dreamed) I shut the door quickly and pretended I hadn't seen.

WHEN I VISITED MY FATHER we always did interesting things. He took me to the studio where his commercials were produced, and let me stand under the lights to feel how hot they were. He introduced me to cameramen and soundmen and directors, and they tousled my hair or solemnly shook my hand. Either way, I felt mocked. I felt ridiculous—Gary Bradley has a daughter, what a joke. We also went to museums, to the zoo, to the park; we ate in restaurants and bought fancy, rich Danishes at Zabar's for breakfast. Sometimes we went to FAO Schwarz and he bought me expensive presents. I listened carefully whenever he talked to other people—salesladies, people on the phone, the man at the newspaper stand, the superintendent of his building. I was listening for that same charming, assured tone he used on TV: Don't you worry, Mrs. Jones, I have just the thing to take care of that. But he sounded different in real life.

THE DAY OF THE FIT—that's how I remember it—we were walking down Seventh Avenue. It was a clear autumn day. My father walked blithely along, looking around at everything. Sometimes I was afraid he forgot about me; I was afraid somebody would grab me and haul me away before he noticed. Then he would say, Look at that, or Are you hungry? and I would be brought back safely into his realm.

We crossed the street. A small crowd had gathered around a man who was lying in the middle of the sidewalk. I wanted to look but turned my head quickly away, as I had been taught to do: Don't stare, don't go near people who are sleeping in the street. My father glanced over. We started walking away, but then he stopped. "Just a minute," he said. "Wait here. Don't move from this spot. I'll be right back."

I stood frozen. I watched him, horrified, as he strode over to the crowd. People stood back to let him through, as if he belonged there. I heard his voice, the authoritative sound of someone in command. I could see now that something was terribly wrong with the man on the sidewalk. His body was jerking. His eyes were white. Saliva bubbled on his lips like toothpaste foam. My father took off his coat and placed it under the man's head so it wouldn't bang on the cement. I was afraid. I was afraid of this man, lying on the sidewalk, convulsing and jerking like that. I didn't want my father touching him. What was wrong with this person? What would happen if he jumped up and started running after me? What would my father do then?

Time moved slowly. The man's fit lasted only a minute or two, but it seemed like much longer. When he stopped jerking, my father asked someone in the crowd for a handkerchief and wiped the man's mouth. Then the man woke up. My father spoke to him quietly, and after a few minutes he sat up and nodded. He saw my father's coat and picked it up and shook it and gave it back, then stood up slowly. The two men talked for a minute, shook hands. My father patted the man's shoulder. Then he came back to where I was standing. He nodded at me, as if we were acquaintances passing in the street, and we began walking. I knew better than to ask what was wrong. I didn't even dare look back at the man who had been doing that awful thing in the middle of the sidewalk, in the middle of the day.

My father glanced down at me. "Epilepsy," he said. "The man was having an epileptic fit."

I frowned, still looking straight ahead, trying this new word out in my head. Ep-i-lep-tic. It didn't sound like anything I had heard of before. Epileptic fit. The words were as crisp as the new dollar bills my grandmother sent with my birthday card every year.

"Do you know what that is?" he asked.

I shook my head. I felt that sense of shame that I got whenever somebody started talking about things they weren't supposed to. The last time somebody had asked me if I knew what something was we were discussing sperm, and my friend Jessica told me things I definitely did not want to know.

"I roomed with a man in college who had epilepsy," my father continued. "They just start convulsing like that. Usually there's a warning. They feel it coming on, and they lay themselves down as quickly as possible so they don't crack their heads open on the ground."

I was amazed. He talked as if there were a whole population of these people having these fits everywhere they went.

"The main thing is, sometimes they can't breathe. They choke. You have to be sure they don't swallow their tongues. My college roommate had this plastic thing—it was thin at one end and thick at the other end so you could slip it between his lips and pry open his teeth, and then he'd be biting down on the thick part. The thing had these teeth marks like you wouldn't believe."

Pry open their mouths? Swallow their own tongues? I gulped, suddenly aware of my own tongue large in my mouth, wondering how in the world you could get your tongue far enough down your throat to swallow it. Did it come off when you swallowed? My father glanced down at me again. "You okay?"

"Yeah," I managed. "It's just—weird."

"They have medicine they can take. But sometimes, like with my roommate, the medicine just cuts back on the number of seizures. It didn't cure him altogether. He had a couple every month, I'd say. Maybe more. I don't know about that guy," he said, nodding toward the place where the man had been lying on the sidewalk. "I don't know whether he was taking medicine or not."

He shrugged and we continued our walk, but I wasn't noticing the beautiful day or the people around me. I wasn't even afraid of being kidnapped or losing my father. I was afraid of strangling on my own tongue.


I DIDN'T TELL MY MOTHER ABOUT EPILEPTIC MAN. I felt my father had been brave and compassionate, but I wasn't sure my mother would see it in the same way. I began to feel an awe for my father, who knew about these fits, who had spent a year in college sticking something like a shoehorn into someone else's mouth, who understood this ugly thing enough to be matter-of-fact about it. There were so many things I didn't understand.

I began to see my parents as two separate, different people, who really had nothing to do with each other. When I tried to imagine my mother helping Epileptic Man, I could only get her to call the police. She wouldn't get near him. In real life maybe she would have. But I couldn't see it happen in my head.

When I watched my father in the detergent commercials and the floor wax commercials, charming these housewives with his lemon-fresh-scent products, I remembered the way he slipped his expensive jacket underneath the epileptic's jerking head, to protect it from the concrete. I remembered him wiping the foamy saliva from the man's mouth. And then a strange thing happened. I began to feel jealous of Epileptic Man. I began to wish that I would have an epileptic fit. I imagined my father slipping his tailored coat beneath my head, wiping my mouth, patting my shoulder. At school I traced the word "epilepsy" on my knee with my index finger. I daydreamed: I was lying in the middle of the street, having a fit, my head hitting concrete with each convulsion. And then my father came along and rescued me. Sometimes he did not.

DURING THAT TIME I PRIDED MYSELF on being able to sneak into the house so quietly my mother didn't even know I was there. It was a game I played. I played it outside, too, in the woods behind our house. I read those stories about Indians and how they walked in the forest without making a sound. I practiced walking on twigs and dead leaves, but they crackled and crunched beneath my feet no matter how carefully I trod. At school, walking down the hall with a pass for the girls' room, I stayed close to the walls. I listened to the voices from other classrooms and crept down the shiny corridor on my white Keds. The smell of disinfectant and floor wax filled my head. My heart beat fast; I felt a stirring in my bowels. Nobody knows where I am, I thought. There was nobody in the halls, nobody in the girls' room, nobody to see me. If I slipped away it would take time for people to notice. I looked at myself in the mirror, wondering if there were times when I became invisible, willing myself to do it now.

On a Saturday morning after The Fit, I sneaked into the house. I was supposed to go to my father's that day, but he had to cancel. "Next week, I promise," he said. "Okay, next week," I agreed. I saw the woman from my dream, the red smiling mouth, and then she was gone.

Outside, I circled the house, staying low near the windows so my mother wouldn't see me. At the front of the house there was a storm door with a metal handle, and a big wooden door with a brass knocker. By opening the door very slowly, I kept the knocker from making any noise. Once inside I was safe; the front room was thickly carpeted. I left the door opened and listened for my mother. There was silence for a moment and I wondered if she was gone. Then I heard her voice—she was on the telephone in the kitchen.

"I have no idea. Except that now he's actually got an apartment. I mean, he's moved there—not like that studio he kept for the occasional late night, when he didn't want to drive home. Or not so occasional, I guess. At any rate, he won't say whether it's permanent. I suppose I should make him tell me, one way or the other. But I can't. I'm too afraid of what he might say."

My eyes widened. I wasn't supposed to hear this. In fact, I didn't want to hear this. I walked back to the door, avoiding the creaking places in the floor. There was a pause, and then my mother said, "Well. This marriage has always been conducted by fits and starts."

The sentence had a rehearsed quality to it: "This marriage has always been conducted by fits and starts." Maybe she had read it somewhere, and was repeating it from memory. I touched the metal handle of the storm door, pushing it slowly until it clicked open, holding my breath to see if my mother had heard me. Then I slipped outside, shutting both doors carefully. I jumped off the front steps and ran through the backyard and into the woods as fast as I could.

Fits and starts. I didn't know what this meant, exactly. I liked the way it sounded, like a whisper, or a hiss. A marriage conducted by fits and starts. Fits and Starts could be names, like a comedy team. Was one of these the husband and one the wife? Mr. Fits and Mrs. Starts. I imagined a man walking around having fits like Epileptic Man and a woman next to him, holding his jerking arm, walking perfectly upright. Then I changed it to Fits and Starch. Fitsnstarch became one person. Someone who was starchy and proper most of the time, but occasionally went wild and had fits. I imagined myself becoming that way. I wondered what my parents would do then.

I stayed away for hours, then banged the door shut so my mother would know I was there. She was in the kitchen making dinner. The table was already set, but the chair my father usually sat in was gone. Later, I discovered it upstairs, in the attic, along with the clothes he left in their closet and the books he kept by their bed. She seemed to have forgotten about the fits and starts. She was humming to herself as she dropped a bag of frozen peas into boiling water. Still, there were dark half-moons under her eyes that didn't used to be there. The skin across her cheekbones looked looser. I sat at the table, playing with the silverware, swinging my legs, wondering what would happen next.

NOT LONG AFTER MY PARENTS' DIVORCE, my father remarried. I don't know if his new wife was the dream woman with the red lipstick or not. I was eleven years old then, almost twelve. I pretended I didn't care. I went to the wedding wearing black. I dusted my face with white powder and outlined my eyes in dark eyeliner. It was 1969, so this actually wasn't as strange as it sounds. "You look like you're going to a funeral," my mother said. She couldn't help smiling. I let her fix my hair the way she liked it, enjoying the feel of her hands and the crackle of electricity as she brushed.

I took the train into the city. I had insisted on going by myself. I wasn't afraid of the city anymore, and didn't want to accompany my father to the church. I sat with my hands folded in my lap. A woman with two small blond children sat across from me, and the children stared at me, their wide blue eyes missing nothing. Their mother read a magazine. I wished she would tell them it wasn't polite to stare. They got off at White Plains. The little girl turned back on the platform to look at me through the window. I stuck my tongue out at her as we pulled away, and she started crying.

When the train entered the tunnel leading into Grand Central, I stared at myself in the black window. At home, alone, I could often frighten myself by staring into mirrors and not letting myself look away. I would look and look into my own eyes and say, Who are you? My own reflection, watching me relentlessly, scared me so much I had to leave the house. I stared now at the ghostly face reflected back at me. After a while I took a Kleenex out of my purse and wiped off the makeup.

My father's new wife was young and pretty and smiled a lot. She was a hands model. Her hands appeared in magazine ads, holding boxes of rice or jars of cold cream, or else she modeled nail polish or hand lotion. I had only met her once, and it had been clear that she didn't know what she was supposed to do with me. My father was the host of a game show now. He was famous. She was marrying a famous man. I was the famous man's daughter. That's all it was.

"I'm a model but I'm not famous," she told me the night I met her. We were eating dinner in a French restaurant. "No one ever recognizes me. Not even my hands. But people certainly recognize your father." She smiled at him proudly. He held her hands like delicate glass birds, picking them up carefully from the table and putting them gently in his own. She looked down at them as if they belonged to someone else. "I have to be very careful," she explained to me. "Every night I rub a special lotion into them and wear cotton gloves while I sleep. I wear rubber gloves whenever I have to do anything with my hands. One little mark would ruin everything."

At the church I sat alone in a back pew and listened to them exchange vows. I listened to my father's "I do," the famous voice resonating up to the high ceiling and back again. I watched him slip the gold band over her perfect finger. I wanted to drop to the floor, to pretend I had fainted, to lie there pale and strange, choking on my tongue. But the moment passed; the bride and groom were kissing; their friends broke into wild applause, as if this were some kind of performance. I felt ridiculous, wearing a black witch's dress to this wedding. I felt ridiculous being there at all.

When people began to leave for the reception I found my father in the cloakroom. "Dad," I said. "I don't feel so good. I think I better just go home."

He turned to me, his face full of concern. His eyes took in the black dress, the pale face, the rings around my eyes where the liner had been. "You look like hell," he said, as if I were one of his grown-up friends. He placed the back of his hand against my forehead. Then he said, "I know this is hard for you, kiddo. But it will get easier. You'll see." He hugged me. I hugged him back, but I couldn't say anything. I was thinking about the way my mother put out my breakfast dishes: how they were always there, waiting for me, every morning, even now that I was older and could get them myself. I imagined her setting out the boxes of cereal, the spoon and bowl. I saw her as if I were standing outside the house in the dark, looking into the well-lit rooms, casting no reflection on the glass. She was wearing her pink velour bathrobe. She folded the paper napkin. Placed the sugar bowl where it belonged. Straightened the place mat. For a moment she stood, looking at nothing, twirling her hair thoughtfully. Then she turned out the light. I stepped back.

"I'll be fine," I said to my father, and realized it was true. "Don't worry."

"That's my girl," he said, patting me on the shoulder. Outside the church he hailed a cab and told the driver to take me to Grand Central Station. He gave me money for the cab fare, and some extra. I watched him as we drove away, and he watched me too, each of us growing smaller and smaller until the cab turned down a side street, and we disappeared.

# bust

Nora had never been all that enamored of her breasts. But now that she was about to lose them, she became nostalgic and sad for them, as if they were old friends about to emigrate to another country with no plans of staying in touch. The country where they lived hadn't appreciated them much anyway: Nora's most humiliating adolescent moments were all connected with her breasts, and recalling those moments (the boys who called her flat, the girl who asked her why she bothered wearing a bra, anyway) could still, at thirty-six years old, make Nora cringe. She went through a difficult, self-destructive time in college when, desperate to please, she slept with any boy who showed an interest. It was Eric, junior year—and she thought of him still with fondness, even though he later tried to steal her mother's car—who proclaimed his adoration of her breasts so consistently and convincingly that she came to believe they were worth something. It took a man to do that, a young man bent on thievery, and now another man was about to cut them off, to save her from their disease. That, she reckoned, was the way of the world, and nothing she could do would change it.

A month before the scheduled surgery, however, she got an idea. A friend of hers was dating a sculptor, the friend being male and the sculptor female, and it came upon her in the middle of a typically sleepless night that she should have a bust made—of her bust. The idea felt wicked to her, funny and right in the face of all the absurdity, and she giggled into her quilt, laying her hands tenderly and protectively over her breasts as she often did in bed these days. The next morning she was up early calling her friend, Ron, to get the artist, Deirdre's, number. The parties involved were all agreeable, even enthusiastic, and Nora and Deirdre set up a time to meet the following day.

Nora arrived at Deirdre's house filled with expectations about what a sculptor would be like. She didn't know any artists, personally, just a would-be novelist who never seemed to do any actual writing himself, but knew about people who did, and which writer's colonies they had been invited to, and which prizes they had won. Nora herself was a veterinary assistant, which mostly meant stool samples and neurotic cats. She liked her job well enough and, after a second divorce (she hardly counted the first marriage—it had lasted two months), she was content, most days, to come home from work, read, watch BBC mysteries on television, and dig in her garden. She was not lonely, or not very much. Still, she found herself wishing that George, her second husband, hadn't hightailed it quite so quickly out of their conjugal life. She could've used his culinary talents and foot massages—though she didn't miss his shopping network problem, nor the resulting credit card debt.

Deirdre was not what Nora expected. Almost conventional looking, she had sleek well-cut hair, a fine sharp nose, and a wide smile with a small gap between her two front teeth. She looked like the type of well-cared-for, middle-aged woman you'd see chatting up the produce guy at the supermarket, searching for an extra-fresh bunch of radicchio. She tossed her head back when she laughed—an expression Nora often read in books. In Deirdre, the gesture was true. And she had the kind of round, high breasts that Nora had always coveted. They were shown to special advantage in a champagne-colored cotton knit T-shirt, tucked into faded Levis. Her feet were bare, and the only artsy accessory she wore was a toe ring on each pinky toe.

"Nora!" she said now. "I've got so many friends who are survivors—you must let me hook you up with a support group of terrific, life-affirming women I know."

Nora smiled, accepted the embrace offered, inhaled the smell of clay and something else that she couldn't quite identify. Some kind of spice, or cologne? "Thanks. I'm all right, though—I've got a lot of friends who are helping me out." This wasn't quite true. At times like this—though what other time was like having breast cancer?—people surprised you, the ones you thought would stand by you leaving you disappointed, and others you hardly knew rushing to your aid. Nonetheless, Nora couldn't stand the thought of sitting in a circle of folding chairs in a church basement with a bunch of cancer patients, swapping chemo horror stories. It sounded even worse than the discussions among women who had recently given birth—dinner party talk of episiotomies or hours spent pushing made Nora want to launch into a detailed and clinical discussion of how to spay a cat.

"Come, sit, I've made green tea," Deirdre said, leading Nora by the hand into a large open room, windows on three sides—her studio. Partially finished pieces sat on metal stands around the room. They reminded Nora of body organs, with tubes and other strange appendages attached willy-nilly. She hated green tea, hated all the things she was supposed to be ingesting, wanted nothing these days but rare cheeseburgers and black coffee and Guinness Stout and filterless Camels, though she had quit smoking a decade ago.

Deirdre motioned for Nora to sit on a futon covered in bright paisleys. "Living in the light of death, isn't that what they say?"

Nora, whose small stature meant she had to sit forward so her feet wouldn't dangle, put her teacup back on its saucer. "What?"

"The light of death. Is every little moment just precious to you now?"

Nora looked at Deirdre's expectant face. "You mean, because I might die?"

"Well, yes. That's the idea."

"I don't plan on dying. I plan on getting my breasts removed and then I plan on living for a very long time, without them."

Deirdre looked at her for a moment, then laughed a big laugh. "Ron told me—he said, 'Watch out, Nora's very droll, she has a very dry sense of humor.'"

"I'm sorry, it's just—"

"No, don't say another word. It's me, I have no sense of boundaries whatsoever. Ask Ron. I'm always saying the stupidest things to people. So we're going to do a cast, then?"

"A cast?"

"A plaster cast, yes. It will be an almost exact replica of your torso. I've never done a torso before—just faces. But this will be much less claustrophobic." Then she leaned forward conspiratorially. "Gobs of Vaseline are involved. Shall we get started?"

"Today? Right now?"

"Why wait? Unless you have another appointment?"

"No, I have the time," Nora said, but felt uncomfortable, had not imagined embarking on the project so soon.

"Don't be nervous, darling. It's just us here today. I used to have nude models prancing around here day and night—it was like a porn set." She was setting up a work area as she spoke, laying a paint-splattered sheet on the floor and mixing a bucket of plaster. "Most people love it, once they get their clothes off, they never want to get dressed again, I practically have to chase them outside and throw their clothes after them. My work is more abstract now," she nodded toward some of the organ-like objects, "which means fewer naked people."

"Here goes," Nora said under her breath, and pulled off her turtleneck. It was like the doctor's office, except no gown. She stood, waiting, not knowing what to do with her hands.

"Ah, you look gorgeous, such a little thing! Like a sprite, in a Shakespeare play. Has anyone ever told you about your aura? It's purple, with yellow sparks—amazing. Here, will it help if I'm naked too?" Without waiting for Nora to reply, she pulled off her T-shirt, unhooked her bra, and put out her arms as if to say "ta-dah!"

Nora smiled. The breasts before her were glorious, and clearly the products of extensive plastic surgery. She had never been naked with another woman before except in locker rooms. Deirdre's complete ease put Nora at ease, and she stood obediently on the sheet while Deirdre found a king-size jar of petroleum jelly and scooped up a glob with her fingers. "Okay, here's the fun part," Deirdre grinned, the gap between her teeth giving her a slightly demented look. She began coating Nora's neck and shoulders and sides and then circled around to her belly. The studio was quiet. Deirdre's flamboyant self had retreated; she was business-like now, her fingers moving over Nora's skin as if she were going to be required to recreate Nora's body from memory and wanted to get every detail just right. When she came to the breasts, Deirdre asked in a hushed voice that echoed in the high-ceilinged studio, "Which one has the lump, darling?"

"Lumps. Both. Did. They took them out. But they'd be back, if I weren't going to have ..."

"Bastards," Deirdre whispered, but Nora wasn't sure if she meant the tumors or the surgeons. The sculptor's callused fingers tenderly coated each breast in cool jelly. How long had it been since someone had touched Nora's body with anything but clinical detachment? She wept.

"Damned disease," Deirdre said darkly. She began applying layers of plaster bandages to Nora's jellied body, the only sounds in the studio the soft slaps of the wet strips of cloth. This was a whole different Deirdre from the one who had talked about purple auras. When she finished with the bandages, she said, "It's going to take a few minutes to dry. You want a glass of wine?"

"Sure." Nora stood alone in the big room, half-encased in plaster, while Deirdre went to fetch a bottle. She seemed to be gone for a long time. Standing there, among the strange tubular sculptures, Nora began to feel like one of Deirdre's weird creations, half plaster, half human being. She could see the grass and trees and sky outside. She wished she were home.

When Deirdre finally returned she was wearing a pale-blue sweatshirt and smelled of cigarette smoke. She offered Nora a glass of very good Merlot, which Nora drank from her standing up position. The goblet was hand blown, with little air bubbles trapped in its surface, and a sea-green tint.

"So how did you meet Ron?"

"Ron," Deirdre shook her head. "Ron came to one of my openings with his ex-girlfriend, the girlfriend before me."

"Kirsten?"

"That's the one," Deirdre said, tapping the plaster. "When he met me he quickly realized the error of his ways," she smiled. "He bought three pieces before he got the nerve to ask me out. I wasn't too keen at first—I mean, a CPA has never really been my type. But he persuaded me. And he promised to help me out of a tax situation. Did you guys ever date?"

"No. I take care of his beagle when he goes out of town. We used to live in the same apartment building, when I was married."

Deirdre raised her eyebrows slightly, as if to say, we'll have that conversation another time, and I'll look forward to it. She tapped the plaster again. "Okay, I think we're done here." She lifted the cast away from Nora's body. The feeling was like emerging from sand, when someone has buried you up to your chin at the beach.

"Look at this," Deirdre exhaled. "It's so perfect. See, by tomorrow the plaster will harden completely, and I'll cut it, here and here." She pointed. "Add another layer of plaster ... smooth it out ... sand it. Then we'll put on some paint, or bronze, and a coat of polyurethane lacquer ... and voilà! You'll be done!"

Nora was standing, her arms crossed, looking at her plaster self. She had imagined something else when she came here—modeling for an artist who would shape her out of clay—but this was so much better. Here was an imprint of her body as it was, now, at this moment, and soon would never be again. She wanted to touch the damp plaster, and suddenly recalled a circle of pink clay that held her five-year-old handprint, a small hole at the top where a white satin ribbon was threaded through. The disc had hung in her mother's room until her mother's death four years earlier. Now it was in a box marked CHILDHOOD in Nora's attic.

"Thank you," Nora said now, moved not so much by the replica of her own frail body, propped there on the sheet, but by the memory of her mother, who had ended up breastless and womb-less and ovaryless in the end. "I'm not a woman," she had complained shortly before her death. "I'm an old paper towel tube, a hollow thing." Indeed she had an emptiness about her as she sat on her bright floral-print furniture, hands in her lap, the television remote control on the arm of her chair, hair patchy like mangy fur. The doctors cut out everything they possibly could. She died anyway.

"You must be freezing." Deirdre got an orange beach towel from a cabinet under the studio sink and wrapped Nora in it, giving her a quick hug. She took her to a large bathroom where she filled the jacuzzi tub, offered her bottles of scented gels and told her to take her time. Nora did, soaked for almost an hour and scrubbed her greasy skin with fragrant bubbly gel. She dried off and felt reborn, her skin new and soft and perfect. When she went back to the studio, Deirdre was gone, which seemed odd. Nora wrote her a quick note of thanks and left it on her kitchen counter. She drove home feeling exhausted, but as happy as she could feel, under the circumstances.

THE WEEK BEFORE HER SURGERY brought an unfortunate series of amputations to the veterinary office where Nora worked. It was May, high school graduation time, and drunken seniors had side-swiped a number of pets without actually killing them. There were three in all, two dogs and a cat, who had to have various squashed limbs removed, so that Nora went to bed that week to nightmares of animal parts, saw them, in her dream life, scattered across Deirdre's studio floor—paws and soft doggy ears and long striped tails, along with, inevitably, her own tragic breasts.

Nora's surgery was, as they say, a success. She had two breasts—and then she had none. The doctors were pleased with how well everything had gone, checked under her dressing and nodded approvingly, as if the masses of torn and oozing flesh were a good thing. Dressings were changed, morphine was adminis-tered. For Nora it was all a haze of animal parts and hallucinated former husbands coming and going and an unfocused, stoned anx-iety that she had missed an important dinner party. The nurses all looked small and dark, as if she had ended up somehow in some other country, Guatemala maybe, though when she woke up another time they were all northern European and imposing. One nurse looked six feet tall.

"You're very tall," Nora croaked. The nurse was pouring a cup of ice water from the turquoise pitcher next to Nora's bed. She smiled. "Six-three," she said.

"Six feet three inches?"

The nurse nodded. "My dad was almost seven feet tall."

So here she had landed in the land of very tall and very short people, in the land of women with breasts, tending the breastless.

The morphine was very good.


NORA SUFFERED COMPLICATIONS; it never goes quite the way they say it will. There had been damage to some nerve bundles, a consequence of the surgery that nobody had thought to warn her about. She couldn't raise her arms, which meant weeks of physical therapy. Then she had radiation, which meant more fatigue, terrible debilitating fatigue. Neither Deirdre nor the plaster cast of her former body crossed her mind for some time. When she did think about the bust, she wasn't sure she was ready to see her old self, bronzed, lacquered, a thing cut off from its legs and head and arms, like remains washed ashore. She was already so separate from everything. On the days when she could go to work, the dogs and cats she had known for years, regular clients, sensed something different about her. She couldn't calm them the way she once had, and felt impatient with their owners, whose worrying over their pets' health seemed an outrageous, stupid luxury. "They're just animals," she muttered to herself one afternoon. The vet, her boss, overheard her, and shook her head. Nora apologized, but couldn't help resenting the fuss made over (for example) Griselda, an eighteen-year-old Persian cat with a nasty disposition whose owner, an unmarried woman around Nora's age, looked at Nora with drowning eyes every time euthanasia was even obliquely mentioned. "Christ," Nora said to herself, ducking out for a coffee break at the 7-Eleven next door. "Let the poor wretch go."

So she didn't think about the bust until her final radiation appointment. In the lobby of the medical building where her radiologist had his office stood a new addition, a copy of the Venus de Milo, which seemed a terrible choice to Nora, this armless chipped thing serving as official greeter to the sick and maimed. The radiologist assured her that the purchase had been carefully researched, that great art was ultimately comforting to people. "It's a message about the human spirit, how we can endure throughout the ages."

"But there are entire pieces of that person gone, including both her arms," Nora said. Lately she had become contentious, annoyed when people didn't seem to take her seriously. Since her diagnosis—truth be told, well before that—Nora had felt as if she were taking up less and less space, her world becoming narrower and narrower, and she worried that one day she would simply disappear altogether. She called Deirdre that afternoon.

The answering machine picked up, with an announcement about an opening of Deirdre's at the local arts center. The same thing happened the next three times Nora phoned. She left messages but Deirdre did not call back as promised in her manic recording—"Wait for the beep, I'll call you back. Ciao!" After morning clinic one Saturday (an ear cleaning on a docile German Shepherd, vaccinations on three yellow Lab puppies, Griselda back for more blood work), Nora drove to the arts center in hopes of tracking down the elusive artist.

What she didn't expect to find when she walked into the center's exhibit area, a large square white room with perfect blond wooden floors, were her own breasts hanging on the wall. And not just hers, but a dozen others like hers, or not like hers, for that was clearly the point—to offer up the greatest possible variety of torsos, male, female, old, young, fat, thin. One was even pregnant. Nora stood alone among the casts, as motionless as if she were getting yet another mammogram, or waiting for just-applied plaster strips to dry on her small frame. She was shocked, really. She was stunned.

The center's director swept in, a short man with red hair. He kept his head cocked to one side as if trying to drain water from his ear. "Sorry I didn't hear you come in—the bell's broken. Have you had a chance to look at Deirdre Bannister's recent work? It's about to go on tour throughout the region. We're so lucky to get it here first. The Human Form, in all its variety ..."

Nora's cast was a glorious red-gold color, mottled as if by a patina of age. It was exquisite. She had never appreciated the beauty of her form. She had always thought of herself as a nice but inconsequential person, the kind of woman whom men eventually left, the kind of woman whose common sense precluded adventure, the kind of woman who would never be considered spectacular.

"This is mine," she said.

"Yes, a lot of Deirdre's models have come by to take a peek. You wouldn't believe the number of people who come in off the street to ask if she'll do them."

"No, I mean, this belongs to me. This is me, and it belongs to me."

"Weeell—" His head cocked a little further to the side, and Nora wondered if he might tip over. "Not exactly. You were the model, but Deirdre isn't selling any of the pieces, to my knowledge anyway. They're going on a traveling exhibit. As I think I said."

Nora looked at the man. His freckled forehead glistened. A perspirer, she thought. "This was my idea. I went to Deirdre and asked her to make this for me. I want to take it home now."

"You'll really have to take that up with Miss Bannister, I'm sure I don't know—"

"She won't return my calls." Nora lifted a hand toward the cast.

The man's voice dropped an octave. "If you touch the pieces, I'll have to call the police."

"Pieces? No. Not pieces. Just this piece. Just my piece." And she stroked the belly of her cast, looking at the man deliberately as she did it. The cast was smooth, like fiberglass, and, she realized, much lighter than it appeared. The director shifted his weight nervously from foot to foot, his face aflame and oozing sweat. Touching the cast calmed Nora, and she gave it a pat, then turned and walked out. She would not make a scene with this person. He was superfluous. She would find Deirdre, and she would get her bust back.

NORA DROVE BY THE ARTS CENTER and Deirdre's studio many times over the next week, and one day she spotted Deirdre's SUV in the center's parking lot. Deirdre herself, and a man who was not Ron, were loading the casts into her car. A casual intimacy between them suggested sex. Nora hadn't talked to Ron in a month, and she called him now, from the parking lot, on her cell phone.

"Deirdre and I broke up three weeks ago," he said from his office downtown.

"I'm sorry. I guess."

"She blew me off one too many times. It wouldn't have worked out anyway. I'm too left-brain for her."

Nora followed the SUV to Deirdre's house and waited for her to get out of the car. Her bangs were cut short, square, like Cleopatra—not becoming, in Nora's opinion. Deirdre turned, surprised to see Nora stalking toward her. "Darling! How wonderful to see you! I've been meaning and meaning to call. Miles, this is Nora, the woman I told you about." Miles, tall and bearded and flannel-shirted—definitely right-brained, Nora thought—nodded in her direction, then went around to the back of the car to begin unloading.

"Come in and have some tea, while Miles does my dirty work. You don't mind, do you, sweetheart?" She smiled in his direction, like a blown kiss, not waiting for a response.

"Let me show you something," Deirdre said to Nora as they walked into the house. Nora was trembling, working hard to contain her anger. Inside the studio were more casts, in various stages of completion—some still damp, some bronzed—like a small army of demi-soldiers lined up for battle.

"Do you see what you've inspired? You've given me this new project, this new world, populated by these gorgeous creatures."

"I've been trying to contact you, Deirdre. Didn't you get my calls?"

"Darling, I've been so impossibly busy." She lit a cigarette, waved the smoke away from Nora's face.

"I want my bust—my cast. I want to take it home with me now. I'll pay you for it. We never discussed price. But of course I'm willing to pay you. That was always the plan."

Deirdre looked at Nora, took a drag from her cigarette, and smiled as she exhaled. "You're looking so well. You've come through the surgery just beautifully."

"Deirdre—"

"The thing is, darling, it's not for sale. I've already committed to exhibiting the whole lot. It's a complete set, don't you see? Taking one away would be like"—she looked around as if the simile she needed were somewhere in the room—"scraping a water lily off a Monet. All the casts have to hang together."

"When will they be back? When can I have it?"

"I honestly can't say when—or if—that will happen."

Nora felt the anger rise in her. This was bullshit. "Deirdre. I came to you, I commissioned you—"

Deirdre stubbed out her cigarette in a seashell-shaped ceramic ashtray. She looked at Nora coldly now. "You've got nothing, my dear. Nothing in writing. I made the piece. So technically it's mine to either keep or sell. And I'm keeping it. I'll let you know if I change my mind." And she strode out of the room, leaving Nora shaking with rage.

As she drove away she saw Miles carrying her cast—its red-gold color a flag beckoning to her—into the studio, tucked casually under one arm like a baguette or a newspaper, and she wept anew at her loss.


THE NIGHT NORA CHOSE TO RETURN TO THE STUDIO was moonless and starless. Deirdre, she had learned, was out of town for the weekend, visiting friends. Nora had figured on an open window, but an old doggy door in the back of the house offered a better route. Once inside, she didn't turn on any lights, afraid the neighbors might notice. She felt her way down the hallway until she reached the studio, where normally the windows would have offered even some dim light, but tonight there was almost none—

just a purple glow from a streetlight. Deirdre's scent, mixed with the clay and plaster and paint and turpentine, hung in the still air. Nora paused, trying to get her bearings. She tried to picture what the room looked like on her last visit, but everything would have changed now. She remembered Deirdre telling her about her purple, sparky aura. In this light, she could almost see that magic as she stretched out her hands and began carefully touching the casts that lay on the floor. She moved slowly down the line, a blind person identifying the dead, brushing her fingers against the bloated bellies of the fat or pregnant people, feeling a squat penis, the bend of an elbow, chests and breasts and partial necks of varying sizes and widths. She had never done anything like this before. Breaking and entering was the phrase that kept repeating itself in her buzzing ears—though she hadn't actually broken anything, at least not yet, had only done the entering part. She continued along on her hands and knees from cast to cast, the purple light flying off her fingers, the bright sparks flying, until she grasped what was familiar.

Nora held the cast against her, cupping her hands over the plaster breasts. They were hard, of course. But the shape was right, the gentle curve. She stood still for several moments, the other casts gathered attentively around her. She didn't feel the triumph she had expected—there was no victory in stealing this detritus. She wished Deirdre would storm into the room, home early from her trip, and they could fight. They could fight and talk and disrobe. Deirdre would want to make a cast of her scarred chest, she was sure. Before-and-after pieces. They would smoke cigarettes and drink beers as they worked. They would discuss the intimate details of their middle-aged lives.

Now she was not afraid of turning on the light. Now she wanted to be caught. She tried on some of the casts, became a sumo wrestler with sagging genitals, a pregnant woman with pendulous breasts, a teenage boy with perfect abs. She began arranging clusters of the casts together, some leaning against chairs, some freestanding, a whole room of mingling half-people having the time

of their lives. In the kitchen she found Russian vodka in the freezer, viscous, almost syrupy, and a dozen round limes in the plastic
egg container of the fridge. The clean citrus smell as she sliced the
fruit reminded her of islands. Nora distributed drinks and ash-
trays, loaded up the five-disc CD player with bluesy jazz, and
raised her vodka in a toast to the torso people. Then she pressed
her own cast tightly against her chest and stepped, armored, out
the front door and into the inky night, into the firefly-spangled
night, into the darkness.

# luck

Teri was sick. Food poisoning, maybe. Those huevos rancheros.
She lay on the king-size bed. They were in Vegas for the weekend,
their anniversary. Jeff was in the casino. He came to see her a while
ago, after she'd vomited for the eighth or ninth time. He was up
six hundred dollars. She was too sick to care about the money, but
it impressed her that he left the table to see how she was doing.
She hung on to that for a while, then passed out again.

Now it was much later. She wished he would come back. The
air conditioner was on too high, and even with an extra blanket
from the closet she was freezing. The clock radio by the bed said
3:21. She lay there for a long time, considering whether the numbers 3, 2, 1 meant morning or afternoon. The drapes were drawn
tight and the only light in the room came from the bathroom. She
finally settled on morning.

The door opened at 7, 4, 9. Jeff brought with him a rush of
smells, cigarettes and scotch and sweat, as well as a styrofoam cup

of coffee with, Teri knew, eight packets of sugar in it, no cream. "Hello," she said, in a croaky voice. He turned the dresser light on. He sat in the chair. He put the coffee on the table. Teri watched him from under the crook of her arm, which she was using to protect her eyes from the light. She cleared her throat. "How much?"

He rubbed his face. It was a handsome face, an Irish face with Irish charm. He lit a cigarette. "I lost the six hundred."

"And?"

"And another twelve hundred. Give or take." He smiled weakly. "Thought I'd quit while I was ahead." She could hear in his ragged voice that his drunk was about played out.

Eighteen hundred dollars. "Is it morning or night?"

"Morning, I believe." He slurped the coffee, then put out the cigarette and lay down next to her. She forgot to tell him to turn off the air, but his body heat would warm her.

She pictured Nathan at home. He'd be getting his own breakfast, his own coffee, which he took light, no sugar. Nathan was Teri's son by a different man, a man she had known when she was young. (He had also been a drinker, but not a gambler. He was a drinker and a pothead.) Teri always got up early with Nathan. She loved their mornings together, the two of them in the warm kitchen, sharing the ashtray and the newspaper and a plate of eggs. Next month Nathan would graduate, start classes at the votech, move into his own place. She could hardly think about how much she'd miss him.

Jeff had been a good daddy to Nathan, but he had a hard time keeping a job. It wasn't just the drinking. Teri had sensed it when they were first together, living in a duplex on Fourteenth Street, next door to those people with the rottweilers. He was lazy. He didn't want to work. Drinking was his excuse. Teri had overlooked the downside because when they met she was twenty-two with a four-year-old son and a job as a housekeeper at the Super 8, and all she wanted was to get married and stay home and raise her kid. Eventually she earned her GED, took night classes at a secretarial school, and landed a good job with the pipe and steel company. Jeff was the one who ended up staying home.

Now Teri lay next to Jeff in their hotel room, on the day after their anniversary, lay there very carefully not saying, What about Nathan's graduation present? She got up, slowly, her legs weak and rubbery. She showered and brushed her teeth, slowly, everything slowly. In the suitcase she found underwear, jeans, a black T-shirt. She looked like shit, like one of those used-up women you see at bus stops in small cities—waitresses or assembly line workers going home after a long day on their feet.

"I'll go see what I can do," she whispered. He grunted, half asleep. She had always been lucky at blackjack. She didn't play often because she felt superstitious about it—that her luck was finite, that she'd been born with just a certain amount and sooner or later she would run out. She thought of the used Mustang on the lot. She had a hundred dollars in her cosmetics bag. She kissed Jeff on the forehead and went downstairs.

She sat at a twenty-dollar table next to a large black man wearing a magenta running suit. The dealer was a red-haired boy who reminded Teri of her son. She ordered club sodas and watched the cards. In an hour she was up nine hundred dollars. By the time she got to twenty-seven hundred, a few people were standing around her table, cheering her on. She cashed in her chips and wrapped the money inside a cocktail napkin, then tucked it into a pocket in her purse. Back in the room she packed the suitcase and woke up Jeff. It was noon and hot when they left the hotel.

"So how'd you make out?" he asked. They were riding the shuttle bus to the airport.

She looked out at the desert, the empty sky, the road leading away from the hotels and the high hopes and the high stakes. She took his hand, but kept her eyes on the highway.

"Not so good," she said.

# bones and flowers

My ex-mother-in-law insists upon buying me a few drinks. My divorce from her son has just come through, and she feels we should celebrate.

Sophie and I have been friends from the start. She is nothing like my own mother, and nothing like me. She is nothing like her son, whom she claims was a changeling child, switched at the hospital by an evil nurse named Kendra. She says her real son is a local poet who occasionally publishes some of the better stuff in *The New Yorker.* He has also appeared in *The Atlantic Monthly,* once. She has followed the name from his debut in a now-defunct Arizona magazine, and in her mind she has created an entire life for him. She thinks he and I should marry.

Her actual son is a dentist. "No soul," she tells me. "Alexander has no soul. He is in a profession that has no soul. A dentist. My god. A man whose main purpose in life is persuading people to floss." She pinches the bridge of her nose and shakes her head in mock disgust. She is joking, at least in part. She loves Alex; she just finds him dull. She thinks he has deliberately rejected his upbringing—liberal private schools, hippie sleepover camps—to get back at her for being what he considers Bohemian. Her solo yearlong trips to Indonesia and Africa. Her wool socks and hand-made sandals. Her bright clothes and unpopular causes. He hates it all. He's a reactionary.

Alex is what most mothers want in a son; what most women want in a husband. He is, among other things, respectable.

He is what I wanted in a husband. Or seemed to be. All those adjectives that my friends and I exchange over coffee, over lunch, over drinks. Caring, kind, strong. Words that slip out of our mouths like soap bubbles, float over our heads, catch the light in just the right way (pinks, blues) before bursting. My friends were envious that I had found such a man. He's perfect, they said. The perfect man.

Alex and I were married for four years. I try to think of him as another stage of my education: four years of high school, four years of college, four years of Alex. He seems to fit nicely into this scheme of things. I try to think of my marriage as a learning experience.

"That's the best way to deal with it," Sophie agrees. We are sitting in a bar that looks out over a golf course and a lake, but beyond that, you can see the Arizona desert shimmering ominous-ly with heat. It's three o'clock in the afternoon and the place is empty except for this guy who looks like Vincent van Gogh (hol-low cheeks, startled eyes) sitting near the jukebox. He is having a passionate and involved conversation with someone sitting across from him who is not really there, and Sophie and I are both fasci-nated with this. The man's mouth shapes his words, but no sound comes out. From his facial expressions, which are as clear and large and specific as an actor's on the stage, we can trace the evo-lution of his emotions: amusement to confusion to anger to rage to shame to embarrassment to sadness.

"For instance," I say, looking away from the crazy man. "I'll never again misconstrue tolerance for love, or a furrowed brow for sensitivity." We laugh, but I feel a tension in my throat.

"He might at least have cheated on you with some imagination. His hygienist. How sickeningly predictable. A boss and his secretary." Sophie makes a face.

"What would you have preferred?"

"Oh, I don't know. Anything but that. What was her name, for god's sake? Something awful. Bunny, or Trixie—"

"No, it was Hannah. She just looked like a Trixie. Someone who would make little hearts over her *i*'s, or circles, instead of dotting them."

"Exactly. Tight uniform, bleached hair. How seedy. Why not some striking woman—a Gwyneth Paltrow look—someone you'd meet at a wine-tasting event? That would fit in with Alex's style."

"Alex doesn't go wine-tasting."

"He should. He does everything else. *Wall Street Journal*, StairMaster, high-fiber breakfasts."

The crazy man near the jukebox throws his head back, holding his stomach and laughing, silent, like a mime.

Sophie and I look at each other and giggle.

"You could marry him," she says. "Never a dull moment."

"I don't want to marry anyone, ever again," I say seriously. "I mean it. I'm going to get knocked up and campaign for day care rights."

"That sounds dreadful. Worse than marriage." We are quiet for a moment. "I'm really sorry, Emily," Sophie says softly, looking into her gin and tonic. I look into mine, as if to read my response, but there are no words there, and I realize I'm going to cry. Sophie motions to the bartender, who is busy with a clipboard. "Two more," she says. Then she puts her arm around me and kisses my cheek; her wild kinky hair smells of baby shampoo and cigarette smoke, and I breathe in the scent thankfully, as if it might save me.

I CAME HOME EARLY ONE DAY from the art gallery where I work and found Hannah in bed with my husband. My bed, my husband. The watery shades of grey I had been seeing for months separated into solid blacks and whites, coagulating right before my eyes. For months and months I had been hanging on and hanging on, in spite of all the signs of decay, all the signs of love gone wrong. It was something in my genes, I know. Family traits: pride, stubbornness. But now there was this—evidence, and I stood there in the bedroom, looking out the window, amazed at how things sometimes went. The neighbor's sprinkler was on, water flashing in the evening sun. As if one could fight something like that, I thought. As if, with our oases of bright green lawns and new adobe houses, we could beat back the desert that creeps up to our fenced-in yards, always threatening to take over. Hannah, clutching my pillow to herself, whimpered and apologized and slunk off to the bathroom.

I watched the light as it fell across the desert in diagonal sheets, tangible geometric planes of Cezanne light, and I kept watching as Alex shut the front door and Hannah's car started and Alex came back down the hall to deal with me. That's the way he saw it, I know. Time to deal with Emily. I could feel him standing behind me, leaning against the door frame, could feel him bracing himself against whatever I might say or do.

But I wasn't thinking about the next step. I was picturing our neighborhood the way it would look from an airplane. I was seeing the brown, dry, cracked earth, dotted with cactus, engulfing the blocks of white and green; I was imagining all of Arizona, divided into pieces of desert and not-desert, the fragile line of square houses forming the boundaries that separated the two. I wasn't thinking about Hannah, or Alex, or myself. I was thinking about deserts, and thinking about lawns.

"It's amazing, isn't it, the conditions that human beings can survive in," I said. My voice was so calm it made Alex jump a little. He expected violence, tears, storms. He expected the sky to darken and the lightning to slice across it in jagged and angry lines. He expected thunder to shake the house, rain to flood the driveway, wind to tear at the sycamore tree in our front yard and strip it of its leaves. And the electricity going out, and the candles lit, and the dinner cooked on a camp stove, and the Chardonnay light and dry, and the kisses heavy and wet, and the wife, finally, full of forgiveness, taking upon her his guilt, relieving him of his burden. Isn't that what couples do? Isn't that what people do for each other? Isn't that the point?

But right then it was all black and white, and I didn't really think about any of this until much later. Right then, the fuzzy greyness that clung to the edges of my vision like mold had disappeared. It was easy. No need to explain. It was clear. Hannah— with the bleached hair and dark roots, with the purple eyeshadow that filled the arch of her over-plucked eyebrows, with the breasts as large as honeydews—was only one way of seeing the light.

SOPHIE AND I FINISH OUR DRINKS, but we do not leave the bar. The crazy man has his elbows on his knees. He is leaning toward his invisible companion, pleading for something. Justice, understanding, love. Maybe he is asking a favor, maybe he needs money, maybe he is in trouble. He leans back, closes his eyes, sighs. He has been denied.

"I'm getting depressed," I say.

"I have some good news," Sophie says, trying to cheer me up. "Colin has just published his first collection of poems." Colin is Sophie's poet-son, her made-up son, the son she has never met. "I saw it at the bookstore. You can imagine my surprise." She pulls out a thin hardcover from her bag and hands it to me so that I see the back first. She does this so I will look at the photograph on the dust jacket. The man she thinks I should marry. It is a black-and-white shot, and the lighting emphasizes large, intelligent eyes, sharp cheekbones, a sad, full mouth. I read the copy below the picture: "Colin Forsythe is a native of Arizona. His work has appeared in many prestigious literary magazines. This is his first book."

"He lives in Tucson now," Sophie says, raising her eyebrows. "The woman at the bookstore says he's giving a reading at the university tonight." She watches me carefully, waiting for a reaction. She is convinced that Colin and I were made for each other. She wants us to try.

The crazy man gets up and walks out the door. His companion has apparently stormed out without warning, and he is following.

I turn the book over and read the title: *desert life*, it says, in small dark letters. Then I look at the picture below the words. A Georgia O'Keefe cow skull, white and cracked, next to a blooming cactus that explodes in pinks and reds like a sunset. A hieroglyph, I think.

I take the dust jacket off and hand the book to Sophie, and she smiles. She knows this is a signal. She knows I will go to the reading with her. And she'll let me keep the bones and flowers, thinking it's the poet's face I want.

# delivery

The new refrigerator arrived at the same time as the phone call, and for a moment Elise was caught between the two responses required of her, unsure of which transaction to complete. She had arranged the morning carefully, put the baby down for an early nap, set the other children in front of an Elmo video, emptied the old refrigerator of its contents, which were now lined up on the counter, kitchen table, and floor. But she never could have anticipated this particular interruption.

"Oh my god, Lee," she said now. "Hang on—I'm sorry, the refrigerator guy is here, let me just let him in." Her heart was pounding. News! Something interesting was happening! It was awful of her to think such a thing, but she couldn't help it—she was already imagining how she'd tell her husband, already anticipating the shape her week would now take. She would make Vicky the apricot chicken casserole. Was it appropriate to bring dinner at a time like this? You always needed food, and Vicky, with her full-time loan officer job and her three kids, surely she could use a meal. Elise beckoned the delivery man into the house, pointed to the kitchen, shushed the children who had, as usual, chosen just the worst moment to announce their dire need for a snack. Did they ever stop eating?

"Lee? I'll have to call you back. It's chaos around here, as usual. If you do talk to Vicky again, tell her I'll call her later, okay? I can't imagine how she's feeling right now." She pressed the off button on the portable phone and for a moment heard her own voice, and wondered. Did she used to sound so—what? Breathy?

The news raced around her entire body, like an electrical current. And when she had a moment—after showing the refrigerator man the basement, where the old fridge would go ("our beer fridge," her husband had already dubbed it)—she felt genuinely sorry for Vicky. She was ashamed for welcoming this drama into her life, and wanted suddenly only to be of comfort to Vicky, who wasn't a close friend, just someone at the edge of their larger social circle in their small college town. Vicky's husband James was a professor—a novelist—and their oldest son was best friends with Elise's. The families had gotten together a few times, but Elise's husband, Kurt, hadn't liked James much, hadn't even liked his name, which, he said, was the usual arrogant academic nonsense. Why not Jim? Kurt wanted to know. What the hell was wrong with Jim? Elise suspected it was a class issue; Kurt had never finished college, and in this town that was a bigger deal than it might be elsewhere. Elise had finished—she had a degree in sociology—had worked for six years as a sales clerk at a department store cosmetics counter before quitting to stay home with her children. Most of the women she knew had made the same choices she had made; that's why they were friends. Vicky's choice, to work full time, would now, Elise knew, be analyzed all over again by the stay-at-home mothers. Maybe if she hadn't been so focused on her career, they would say. Maybe if she had been home more.

Still, Vicky was lucky, wasn't she? If James really had left her for an undergraduate—a nineteen-year-old!—if it wasn't just temporary insanity, then Vicky was right to have made a career for herself. She'd need it now, if you could believe those articles on divorce. What were the chances that James would support three kids on to college? Nil. Elise felt a stab of real sorrow for Vicky—how humiliating the whole thing was!—and then the boy in charge of the delivery called out to her.

The boy in charge wore a baseball cap and a faded red T-shirt and jeans. His two helpers did the heaviest work: one short black guy, one short white guy with a face oozing acne. They'd moved the old refrigerator, and now the boy in charge was alerting Elise to the crud—the stuff left behind on the floor. Did she want to clean there before they brought in the new refrigerator? She hadn't cleaned under there for a while, well, maybe ever, and the gunk was considerable. She swept away the long-ago lost plastic magnet letters, three Legos, a hair tie, a roach trap, then began scrubbing. The boy marked things on a clipboard while the other two brought the new refrigerator into the house in pieces, one side door, then the next. She was conscious of cleaning on all fours, wearing her skinny jeans—she still looked all right, in spite of the toll the babies had taken on her, but she knew how this boy must see her: his mother. Well, that was all right with Elise. This is who she was, forty years old last year. The mother of four—four!—children. A mother whose own mother had disappeared when she was six, abandoned her, and that fact followed her closely around every day, poking its nose here and there, was she doing this right, was she being a proper caretaker to her children, was she going to be found out for a fraud. A woman surrounded now by perishables: mayonnaise, pickles, mustard, grape jelly, half-full jars of spaghetti sauce, eggs, old Cool Whip containers filled with taco meat, cooked rice, other forgotten and undoubtedly moldy leftovers.

Before the delivery men left, the boy in charge, in his slow farm-boy way, pointed out some problems with the new refrigerator. Elise, he said, could call the store about it. The door on one of the special compartments didn't shut all the way, he demonstrated. The refrigerator door itself didn't close automatically, with a push—it had to be firmly shut. Something about the leveling. There were other instructions, for the icemaker, for the water filter. Elise was afraid she wasn't listening closely enough. Kurt was a stickler for such details. He would want a full report.

So she called the store—she hated stuff like this, how could a twelve-hundred-dollar refrigerator, brand new, have so many problems?—in between tying Superman capes on the children and finding the apricot chicken recipe for Vicky. "She's in shock," Lee had said. "She had no idea this was going on." Not until the girl herself called James at home, and Vicky had answered. "Mrs. Randall," she had said, "could you please have James call me?" Vicky, assuming she was a student needing an appointment for a conference or clarification on an assignment, assured her she would. "And what's your number?" "Oh—" a little laugh. "He knows the number." "I see," Vicky said, and hung up. James arrived home a few minutes later, and Vicky said, hoping she was kidding, "Your girlfriend called." He looked stricken. Sat down. "Shit," he said. The last of the smooth operators, Lee said.

The affair had been going on since Christmas; it was now April, almost the end of the semester, and certainly the end of the marriage. This was the second affair—the first had been more reasonable, with a woman student closer to his own age, a graduate student with one divorce and two children of her own under her belt. The journey back to the marriage had been long and arduous. Now no such trip would be made. Now they were done with their travels.

James was fifty-two. The girl in question was nineteen.

Disgusting, Elise thought, as she filled up her new appliance, wiping the bottoms of jars with a sponge before placing them on the shiny white shelves, a hint she had read about in a magazine. She called her two preschoolers, three-year-old Sarah and four-year-old Aaron, into the kitchen to show them the icemaker and water dispenser. They cleared out a kitchen drawer and put in their favorite cups; with a stool from the bathroom, they could reach the spout and get their own water. Celebration ensued. Then Joe arrived.

Joe Demory, awash in Old Spice, was a manager of Midwest Appliances, the person Elise had talked to on the phone. He had 1970s hair (parted in the middle, a modified shag), country-music-singer eyes, a moustache. Elise showed him the two plastic pieces the boy in the cap had left behind. He began talking to her about why the two pieces were not put into the doors. It had to do with how level the refrigerator was and the peaks and valleys and whether or not she'd be able to pull the refrigerator from the wall. What she gathered was, if the pieces were installed, she would not be able to pull the refrigerator from the wall, but even that much she was shaky on. Her explanation would not be enough to satis-fy Kurt. She sighed, asked another question, tried to find the phrase in what Joe was saying that would act as a code: Here, Kurt, this is the answer, this is what you need to know. Now can I stop thinking about it? She watched Joe as he talked and realized why she couldn't concentrate. He looked too much like her old boyfriend Howard. Or no, not boyfriend. Howard. She hadn't thought of him in years. How weird, she thought, that he should crop up today, with this Vicky business going on.

She had met him one winter when she had taken some time off from school, worked for a few months as an encyclopedia salesperson. Howard was one of the salesmen she was paired up with to canvass neighborhoods. Howard, like James, was married. One afternoon when the weather was bad and no one was letting them in the door, he kissed her. They sat in his Chevette with the heat blasting, necking. He had soft lips and a small tickly moustache like Joe Demory's and she liked kissing him. To tell the truth, the fact that he was married never really entered her mind. Howard himself didn't seem to feel the least bit of guilt. His wife was part of some other reality, one that did not, apparently, intersect with the reality that Elise inhabited. She realized now—and it startled her—that really, they'd had an affair. Their sex had seemed more like a way to relieve the boredom of their work, to alleviate the sense of failure they often had at the end of another day with no sales. Once, they went through a neighborhood she had never been to before. They parked near a house with a brick walkway and a screened-in side porch. Howard pointed to it and said, "It's empty."

"How do you know?"

"They're on vacation. In Florida. Till Easter."

They canvassed the neighborhood. Most people weren't home. The next day they went back. The houses on either side of the vacationing couple's house were also empty, at least during the day. Howard went around back, and appeared at the front door to let Elise in.

"What are you doing? This is illegal." But he had just pulled her in by the hand and made frantic love to her on the blue wall-to-wall carpeting. They had gone back three more times, then got skittish when they noticed a woman walking her dog and studying Howard's license plates. How old had Howard been? Not as old as James. Probably about Elise's age now. Forty, to her then-twenty.

Joe had finished explaining. Now he was asking her for a lubricant. Petroleum jelly. She walked to the nursery and brought back the Vaseline. Joe dipped his finger into the jar and began coating the strip of refrigerator door that met the rubber, "just a very thin coating," he explained, that would help the door shut. A salesman smelling of Old Spice using Vaseline on her refrigerator—it was embarrassing. She didn't think a coating of Vaseline would satisfy Kurt. She called him on his cell phone, gave him a broken explanation about the refrigerator door, indicated that if the phrase "peaks and valleys" didn't cover it for him then he'd better talk to Howard—to Joe, rather—himself. Elise gave Joe the portable phone and began making grilled cheese sandwiches. The length of the conversation between Joe and Kurt suggested to Elise that she had certainly done the right thing by calling him, because later there would have been a lot of questions and she wouldn't have been able to answer a single one.

She cut the sandwiches in triangles, put them on plastic Winnie-the-Pooh plates, dumped some goldfish crackers on top, and delivered them to the children in the next room. Joe finished the conversation and returned the phone and the jar of Vaseline to Elise. She passed him a paper towel without meeting his eyes. Was he older than she? She couldn't tell about people's ages anymore. It used to be that everyone was older. Now everyone was starting to be younger. Joe was wearing a wide silver wedding band. Maybe he was thirty-two. Maybe he was twenty-six. Maybe he was forty. She remembered, as she walked him out the door, still holding the Vaseline and the phone, she remembered the way her mother had kissed her lightly on the forehead that July morning all those years ago, had walked down the porch steps wearing a pair of bell-bottoms and a fuchsia T-shirt with a neon green head of broccoli silkscreened across the front, had said to Elise, "I'll be right back," as if she really would be right back. Elise had waited on the porch, had waited a long time, until her father came home from his housepainting job and took her inside and gave her a bowl of Lucky Charms.

She started to say something to Joe—something about Vicky, or Howard, or her mother—but caught herself in time. She stood on her front steps watching as he got into his Saturn, adjusted his rearview mirror, pulled out of the driveway. For a moment she could see herself floating out the door, climbing into Joe's car with him, waving out the window at her own children as they stood watching her leave, disbelief and confusion on their faces. I'll be right back, she heard herself call. It was a terrifying image, and she forced herself to go inside and continue putting away the perishable things, wiping the bottoms of the jars as she had learned to do, and placing them where they belonged.

# remembering tom blake

## 1.

He comes upon you suddenly. There is no warning.

Say you're draining the capellini. The clam sauce is perfect. Your lover is wearing that heavy wool sweater you really like, and he's saying something warm and intimate as he opens the wine. You've changed his life, he's never known love like this before. Whatever.

And then, without warning, as you serve the fragile pasta lovingly onto warmed ceramic plates, there he is. Tom Blake. Well, someone else for you, of course. What was it that brought him back this time? The smile of the anchorman on the local news? The way your lover put his hand on the small of your back as he kissed your cheek? Maybe. Or maybe nothing. Maybe Tom Blake just wandered back of his own accord, just popped in to say hello. There is the delicate dark skin of his eyelids, or the way he used to laugh, deep from his gut, or softly into your neck. Or there is his hand, scooping your hair into a clumsy ponytail, holding it while he kisses you. And it takes your breath away, sometimes. I mean it: a sharp intake of breath and maybe even a hand to your heart, or your mouth.

Now when you eat the capellini, you find that it's slightly over-done. On its way from the stove to the table, the clam sauce has become disappointingly cold. You drink more wine than usual. It leaves a sour taste in your mouth.

After dinner, your lover sits next to you on the couch, warm and intimate in his scratchy sweater, and you know he's thinking that you're thinking he looks pretty terrific.

Suddenly, you don't feel so good anymore.

## 2.

FOR ME, IT MIGHT GO LIKE THIS:

I'm eating chicken salad in a restaurant. I'm alone, it's my lunch hour, and I've got a magazine at my elbow. I turn the page, glance out the window. Across the street there is a sign in the window of a liquor store: the familiar blue and white and gold of the Busch Mountains sign.

And there he is. Sitting across from me at a booth in our college bar. I hold a forkful of chicken salad in midair, looking. He's leaning across the sticky table to pour me another beer from a plastic pitcher. He's smiling a little, behind his beard, and shaking his head, and the feeling I have, sitting across from him, is that I want to reach over and touch his thick, brown hair, to feel the weight of it between my fingers. I can see he's wearing a green T-shirt under his plaid flannel, and I want to put my hand there, too—on his chest, under the soft faded cottons of his clothes. He's shaking his head, maybe in self-deprecation, I can't tell. I don't hear the words yet. It's a silent movie.

What I can tell is that this is our first time alone together. I can tell this because we are on our best behavior. Our postures are good. We are practicing an unusual amount of deference. Both of us gesture to pay for the beer. Our eyes are bright and I am worried about my hair. Soon, within minutes perhaps, we will decide to go home together. We will make it clear that this is what we both want. Look how careful we're being to send the right signals. We're watching closely to make sure they are the same.

And the more I think about it, my lunch hour ticking away, the more I want to bring back that moment, that decisive and elusive moment when things shifted between us and we began to anticipate each other. Want, want, want. I want that moment now. I begin to imagine the words, the gestures, the delicious understanding in our eyes. I don't have all the facts anymore, you see, so I begin to make them up.

I hear him say, "I've been watching you, Rebecca. Noticing you for a long time." This almost makes me laugh. Tom would never have said anything like that. I try again. I hear—as if he were leaning over his shoulder from the table behind me and whispering in my ear—"You want to come over to my house for a nightcap? My roommates will be asleep by now."

I shake my head, push my plate away, close my eyes.

And finally, I hear this: "The thing is, I've got a girlfriend back home. Sort of."

And I hear myself say, "Sort of?" I'm smiling, coy, full of encouragement. "I hope that's the operative phrase in that sentence."

And he grins and says, "It is." Which is how we understand what is going to happen next.

**3.**

OR THINK OF THIS:

A small New England college in the mid-1970s, where the men outnumber the women three to one. Cheap birth control pills available at the Student Health Center. No worry about AIDS, or even herpes, not back then. Think of a sensible, smart, relatively attractive person in her senior year at this college. A job as an assistant to the assistant editor at a small publishing company in New York City waits for her after graduation. Her course load for the spring semester is light. She has lots of time to play. Nothing much to worry about. No boyfriend clamoring for, or resisting, commitment. Everything simple and clear.

Think of this woman on a winter night, alone, in a room painted gold in a house on Maple Street in this cold New England town. She is finishing her fourth glass of Scotch and deciding what to do. She pours herself another drink, sees her reflection framed in the dark windowpane, thinks that at this stage of the game things start to feel pretty inevitable.

She decides to go.

Her housemates watch, concerned, as she walks down the stairs and into the kitchen and veers toward the front door. She finds her coat hanging on the back of a chair and puts it on. "Rebecca," they say. "Rebecca, it's freezing out there." But Rebecca pays no attention. She holds her drink and walks carefully down icy front steps and onto icy sidewalk, and slides and skates her way to a different street where a large stone house stands, lights blazing in every room. It is below freezing outside. The stone house looks warm and inviting.

There are large apartments on both floors of this house. Other college students live here. She can see the ones on the first floor, reading and napping and making macaroni and cheese for a midnight snack. That's how close she is, close enough to see the blue and white Kraft Macaroni and Cheese box from where she stands.

But she doesn't care about that. She looks up at the second floor windows, to Tom Blake's window. A faded Indian bedspread with doves and peacocks on it hangs over the glass. In the window next to his there is a lit-up Busch Mountains sign.

She stands there, watching, this person who will graduate cum laude and work for a small but important publishing house in only four short months, this person who has never allowed men to take over her life, but who now thinks of herself as obsessed. A glass of Scotch in one hand, a cigarette burning in the other, she waits, wanting more than anything to walk inside that house and up those cheaply carpeted stairs and into the arms of the one man on campus who has made it quite clear that he can never, ever see or be seen with her again.

It is so cold that her body is shaking violently, but she doesn't notice. Her chattering teeth almost break the rim of the glass as she drinks. She thinks, I am desperate for the love of this man. Imagine! She herself is amazed by this behavior. But she keeps standing there, for ten minutes, for twenty, watching the window on the second floor, sipping her Scotch and cupping her cigarette until it goes out.

There are only two lights in his room, the overhead light and the desk light. The desk light is on but this doesn't necessarily mean he is home. Sometimes he leaves it on, forgetting. All she can see is a small, dull glow.

In the other windows one of Tom's roommates crosses the living room to turn off the TV; another makes a pot of tea in the kitchen. She watches, leaning against a maple tree now, caring less and less about the paper she must write for Victorian Poetry. It is due tomorrow. She hasn't even thought of a topic yet, and while she has never once in her entire academic career asked for an extension, tomorrow will be the day she breaks this impressive record.

"Feel me here, Tom Blake," she whispers. "Think about me waiting for you. Think about me and come outside and we'll go for a walk, we'll go to the bar and have a drink and hold hands under the table. We'll even talk about your hometown honey. Dawn," she says, her nose wrinkling involuntarily. "Or we won't. Whatever, whatever you want. Just come out, just find me. Then it won't matter about my paper," she says. Her voice is louder now. She speaks belligerently. "I'm willing to take the consequences of not doing my paper if you're willing to come out here. I'm willing to make the trade, the sacrifice, the deal." She can hear the drunkenness in her speech, and wonders how much she is exaggerating it. Not much, she thinks. "I'll wait. As long as you want. I'll count to thirty, to three hundred—" But she doesn't bother, knowing that rituals of this sort change nothing. Having learned this on previous nights, for this is not the first hour that she has spent standing in front of this stone house, watching. Oh, no! This sensible, smart person has been stumbling down Maple Street every night for three weeks to stand here, against this tree. Now she swallows the last of the liquor in her glass. Her fingers are numb; she forgot her gloves, but it doesn't matter. She forgot her hat, too, and wonders if the tips of her ears have turned black with frostbite. Doesn't matter. "Who cares?" she mutters to the impervious stone house. "Who the fuck cares? Not you, Tom Blake, you son of a bitch. You insensitive, stupid son of a bitch!"

She looks at his window hopefully.

She remembers: a month ago she pushed aside that make-do curtain and looked out that window, watching a heavy snow fall while Tom Blake gazed at her from his wide, warm mattress. The snow fell so thick she could hardly see the outlines of the church across the street. A pair of nuns made their shadowy way from the parking lot behind the church to the church's front steps, where they yanked on the heavy front doors. Then they turned around and made their way back through the deepening snow. Rebecca started to laugh. She started to say, "There are a couple of nuns out there, locked out of their church!" But Tom spoke before she had a chance.

"I love you," he said. Yes. That morning was the first time he said it. The last time, too. I love you. She had turned from the window, imagining herself in the dim snowy light, glowing white and smooth and lovely, imagining that she must have been transformed by those words. A glance in the mirror over the dresser as she walked back to bed told her she was transformed. She had become ethereal, a Botticelli figure, floating across the floor. She had changed because this time, she wanted something that would last. She wanted love. She wanted Tom Blake.

Don't I have any right to this man? Rebecca thinks, turning her face to the maple tree. She tries to cry but is not the sort of person who cries when drunk. She yells, she curses, she throws things. But she does not cry.

On her way home she takes a detour and stops at a friend's house to buy three white crosses. One of these will shake the effects of the Scotch and keep her awake long enough to invent a paper topic. The other two she will save for next time. She will have to think of a thesis that is complicated enough to impress her professor and warrant a three-day extension. She plans her strategy. "I got started on this last week, and thought I could handle it, but as it turns out this is much more extensive than I originally thought, and I need some more time. I thought I'd narrow the focus by concentrating only on ... *Duplicitous-s-s-s*," she hisses, stomping her feet to bring the feeling back into her toes. She turns, once, facing the direction of the stone house, and hisses the word again. Then she looks down at her feet, wondering why she still can't feel them, and sees that she is only wearing a pair of thin handmade moccasins.

She forgot her hat, her gloves, and her boots. She forgot everything for the sake of Tom Blake.

She holds the empty glass high over her head, then throws it at the blue icy street as hard as she can, listening to the satisfying crash and watching the shards skid across ice and snow and scatter, sparkling, dangerous.

# 4.

WHEN TOM AND I FIRST GOT TOGETHER, his friends came to me and talked. Whenever they found me alone, drinking coffee in the Union or taking a cigarette break in the library lobby, these people I hardly knew sat or stood with me and talked about my new lover. I had never experienced anything like it.

"It's so good to see him finally getting it together. Really. I wouldn't have believed it a few months ago. Since he met you—I mean it. He's changed. His situation back home ... you know," they said, looking at me meaningfully. "She keeps dragging him back. Dragging him down, as far as I can tell. You know the kind of situation I mean." I nodded. I had a pretty good idea. "It's just so great to see him with someone like you." At this point they always stopped, worried they had said too much, or implied too much with that phrase "to see him with," as if: once with, always with. For all they knew, Tom Blake was just a fling to me. Someone to help pass the long cold nights and short grey days. They had to be careful. But I always encouraged them with smiles and nods. "What can I say? He's different." I raised my eyebrows: Tell me more. They did. "He's not spending every free minute drinking beer and getting fucked up. He's actually getting into his classes, he's talking about going somewhere other than back to his hometown after graduation. Which I think would be great. I know it would. He says maybe he'll move to Boston or even New York, maybe interview with some of the firms that come in the spring, to recruit. He's talking ... I don't know. It's like he's finally planning to do something with his life."

Who wouldn't have been encouraged by such talk?

I could only guess what Tom had been like before. Or what he was still like, with Dawn. We didn't talk about Dawn, and all I knew was that Dawn and Tom had dated in high school, and when he left for college they agreed to keep seeing each other. Maybe they had some understanding that no one knew about. In any case,

Tom slept with other women, women he met at school, and either Dawn knew about it and didn't care, or she knew about it and did care, or she didn't know about it at all. No one was really sure. Tom's friends said Dawn wanted to marry him, but back then marriage seemed like an absurdity to me, and when they mentioned it, I laughed.

Once Dawn called Tom while we were lying in bed. This seemed very awkward, and I got up and put on his robe and went to the kitchen. He didn't say anything about it afterwards. I was careful not to complain or ask any questions. It wasn't any of my business, not yet. I could wait.

## 5.

THEN THERE ARE THE COLD, HARD FACTS.

After Tom's declaration of love, he disappeared. A week went by, and no word. Someone said he had gone out of town. He did not call, or write, or leave a message for me anywhere. I tried calling his house twice, but his roommates said they had no idea when he'd be back. Did I want to leave a message? I could picture my phone number scribbled on a matchbook cover, or on the inside of a textbook that happened to be lying near the phone. "No, it's not important," I said.

I can deal with this, I told myself, gritting my teeth. I've dealt with this before.

Still, I looked for him every day. I couldn't help it. But when my friends asked about him, cautiously, gingerly, I snapped at them. "Tom? What the hell do I care where he is?"

"Jerk," they agreed. "He could at least call you." I changed the subject.

Every night at the college bar I sat where I could watch the door, but made a point of not watching. Then one night he was back. He came into the bar, looked around, found my booth, walked over. He asked if he could sit down. I looked at him with as much indifference as I could muster and shrugged. "Sure," I said, finishing my beer. Very cool. My friends slipped out of the booth and widened their eyes significantly. I shrugged at them too. Tom sat. He did not remove his backpack from where it was slung over one shoulder. He was not going to make a night of it. I felt disappointed in spite of myself.

"You want a beer?" I said. "I'm going up for another beer."

He nodded, pulled a dollar from his jeans. When I came back I saw what I hadn't, in my aloofness, seen before. The skin around his eyes was dark, his face was pale. His eyes were glassy. He was exhausted. Something terrible had happened.

"So what's going on, Tom? Where've you been?" I sounded concerned in spite of myself.

"Home. I've been home. I'm sorry I didn't call you or anything. I just couldn't get the nerve up to call."

"What? What are you talking about?" I held my glass of beer with both hands, thinking I might break it if he didn't tell me soon. His speech seemed slower than usual, and I watched his mouth as if to catch the words, one by one, as they dropped from his lips.

"It's Dawn. Dawn's pregnant."

Dawn's pregnant.

Later I would think about those words, and how Tom was already used to the way they sounded by the time he said them to me. He had already said them over and over to himself, and spoken them to other people—his parents, maybe, or his friends. Dawn's pregnant. It was almost easy for him to say, now. Like saying a cliché. Into every life a little rain must fall.

My hand flew to my mouth. Melodramatic, I know, but a reflex nonetheless. "Oh my god," I said. Dawn's pregnant. This was not what I had expected. What had I expected? Nothing about Dawn. I had expected something about us. That he had changed his mind about me. That he regretted saying I love you. He had made a mistake. He didn't love me after all. But that wasn't it, and for a stupid moment I felt relieved. He still loved me! There was a crisis in his life, but he loved me! And nothing really had to change between us. It was too bad, what had happened to Dawn, but I could be supportive, things could continue. I could see myself being understanding for this man, putting up with the situation, dealing with it. Everything could work out.

So I began the process of getting through it. I asked the most obvious question, expecting the most obvious answer.

"So what are you going to do? What is she going to do?"

He drank down half the beer in his glass. "She's going to have the baby."

I stared at him. "She's going to have the baby?"

He nodded. Finished his beer. I looked down at the table, trying to understand what this meant. Keep going, I thought. Don't lose it now. "And what are you going to do?"

"I don't know. I'm not going to marry her, though. I'll stay with her till the baby's born. I have to do that. But I'm not going to marry her." He pushed his empty glass to the center of the table. "The thing is, she'll be spending weekends up here from now on. She'll be staying with me."

"I see. Of course. So you and I—"

He shook his head. After a while he slid out of the booth. "Well. Guess I'll see you around."

"Yeah. See you around," I echoed.

What else? What else could I do?


6.


OF COURSE THERE WAS THE DRAMA, in subsequent weeks, of Tom's predicament. Everyone talked about it. His friends came to me, just as they had before, but now they shook their heads sadly. He had been manipulated by the invincible Dawn, they said. He had been on the verge of breaking up with her, and she found a way to keep him. She stopped taking her pills. She got pregnant deliberately. Duplicitous. They talked about how Tom had almost gotten free. I had almost saved him. He had almost saved me, too. But I didn't tell them that.

I spent a month watching his window. Standing in the cold and waiting for a sign. I never got one. Then one morning I saw him walk into a coffee shop downtown with a woman I knew from my photography class, and after that I stopped going to the stone house. I stopped drinking for a while. I stayed at home at night, and read or slept.Weeks went by. Winter gradually retreated. The snow melted and our campus was transformed. On weekends bands played on the quad while people sat under trees and studied for exams, or played frisbee, or lay on faded Indian bedspreads, sleeping in the tenuous sunlight of a New England spring.

I started going out again. The world had changed while I lived in my gold room, and I began to feel changed myself. I began to look at other men on campus, and to talk to them at parties, and to go home with them afterwards. Tom and I inevitably saw each other at some of these parties. I suppose I made a point of going to the places I knew he would be. It wasn't that I held out any hope for us. I knew very well that his original plans had changed, and that he and Dawn were planning a wedding after all. No real surprise there, when you think about it. But I wanted to see him. I wanted to talk to him. Not with the obsession of my month's vigilance. It was different now. It was as if I had heard about him from somewhere, and I wanted to see for myself that what I heard was true.

Sometimes we flirted. As I bent to fill my plastic cup at a keg of beer, he would lean over and whisper in my ear. My legs would go weak from the things he said, but when I straightened, my cup in hand, we would pretend nothing had happened. Sometimes we danced together, or talked, but more often we just watched each other from across the room. We even watched each other seducing other people, or being seduced by them. And at the end of the night we always watched each other leave. The one at the door would glance over a shoulder and find the other, standing alone or not alone, and either way we exchanged a resigned smile or a half-hearted wave. Once, we even left together. We were standing against a wall, very drunk, and the noise and smoke and the people thrashing around on the dance floor and the smell of beer became suddenly oppressive, and just as I was about to leave Tom said, "Let's get the hell out of here." I remember what a relief the mild clear air was as we walked, arm in arm, to the stone house. Everything was so quiet, so clean. The town was asleep and dark and we felt as if we had escaped something. Maybe we even ran part of the way. I don't remember what we talked about, or if we talked. I'm not sure we even realized what we were doing until we were inside his room. We just went there, as if that was what we always did. Nothing seemed strange about it. I wasn't thinking, Oh, finally, here we are together again. No, we just went to his room and went to bed. To tell you the truth, I don't think we even did anything. I think we just got undressed and lay down and slept, our heads still thick with liquor and noise.In the morning we stayed in bed until noon, not wanting to get up, knowing this was it. Graduation was only two weeks away. There would be no more time for anything like this to happen again.

"Nicholas Hansen?" he asked.

"What are you talking about?" But I knew what he was talking about. He had seen me with Nicholas the week before.

"Did you sleep with him?"

"Yeah, I slept with him," I said. "What about it?"

"Nicholas Hansen!" Tom practically shouted. "Oh my god! You're kidding, you've got to be kidding! Nicholas Hansen!"

"Tracy Rydel?" I retorted.

He groaned and put the pillow over his head. I was stunned. It had been a wild guess. "Tracy Rydel? You didn't really, did you?

Jesus, Tom. Does she get up at six to curl her hair?"

"Five-thirty," he said in a muffled voice. "She gets up at five-fucking-thirty." Then he peeked out from the pillow. "Graham Scot?"

"How did you know about that?" I said, leaning on my elbow.

"Rebecca, Graham Scot! Come on! You could do a hell of a lot better than Graham Scot!" We looked at each other and laughed. "Did he fix you tofu for breakfast? Graham Scot! Was it, like, really a natural experience?"

"Oh shut up. How about—how about that blonde, the one you were dancing with on Friday. If you can call what you were doing with her dancing. You know who I mean. The short one with the punk clothes and the skinny legs and the big tits. What's her name?"

"I'm not telling," he said petulantly.

"But you did! You slept with that little slut! God! I bet you had to sign up on a waiting list for her. In between the Chi Psi's and the football team." We giggled. "So what is it? Bibi? Candy?"

"Actually it's Tamara," he said with fake haughtiness.

"Oh, Tamara. Come on, Blake. What are you doing, sleeping with girls like Tamara and April and Brigitte? You could have slept with me, you know. Instead of running after all those little freshmen. You could have saved yourself a lot of trouble and just slept with me."

I stopped. The room was suddenly quiet. I wondered if Tom's roommates had heard us. He kept looking at me while I looked at the floor. A history book lay open next to the stereo. A plant had fallen over—last night?—and its soil was scattered on the worn carpet.

Tom put an arm around my neck and kissed my cheek. I got up and pulled on the jeans and T-shirt that lay tangled on the floor by his bed before he could have the chance to ask me to go. I found my backpack, my sandals, my hairbrush. He watched me from the long, wide mattress. I took my time, brushed my hair and braided it, looking out the window, hoping for a sign. Something that would give me a hint as to where I might be. But there were no nuns today. No snow. No words of love. No grace in the way I moved or felt. So I slung my backpack over one shoulder, kissed Tom Blake once on the mouth, and walked out the door.

Outside, I lay my hand on the bark of the maple tree where I had spent so many stupid hours. Enough, I thought. Enough.

## 7.

ONE OTHER THING. The last thing I remember about Tom Blake.

A few days before graduation I was walking across campus, on my way to pick up my cap and gown, wondering if I would see Tom long enough to say good luck or goodbye or is there an address where I can send you a Christmas card. I was feeling that safe kind of sadness that you feel when something is over but something new is about to happen, and you know you won't have time to feel bad for long. It's almost a pleasant feeling, really, and I began to feel pleasant and hopeful about my life, and the new job I would start the following week, and living in the city, which I ended up leaving before the end of the year, but who knew, at that point? Everything, then, seemed to be moving more or less in the right direction. And then I saw Tom, walking toward me, his cap and gown on one arm, his pregnant bride on the other. He smiled, waved at me a little. I did the same. My heart was pounding. In another moment, they had passed me, and I walked slowly, already trying to remember how he looked. (All I saw of Dawn was her protruding belly covered in a bright pink smock. I don't even know what color hair she had. I don't even know if she was pretty.)

But Tom. How did he seem? Not sad, or proud, or depressed, or angry, or embarrassed. What was it, then?

Finally it occurred to me. I had seen that look before. I had seen it from across crowded parties and smoky bars. I had seen it in doorways and coatrooms.

He had smiled at me the way he smiled whenever I caught him leaving the party with someone else.

I wanted to shout something after him. I wanted to write him a letter. I wanted to tell him—

Anything. A few words. The things I never got the chance to say. I love you. Good luck. Think of me, Tom Blake. Yes. Think of me as you're heating up a jar of baby food. Or washing the car. Or shoveling snow from your driveway. Let me come back to you all of a sudden, my hand in your thick hair, my breath on your neck, my skin under your fingertips. Let me steal upon you without the slightest warning, and take your breath away.

# beautiful things

The first time it happened it was a surprise, but not really a surprise, like seeing a question on a test in a dream, something you were supposed to know but didn't.

As soon as it happened it was over, so the blur of his hand and the sharp sting on her face and the fast reaching out to hold and steady and then, weeping, embrace her—all seemed like one fluid motion, a stone sailing over a pond and falling in, and then it was gone and you could ignore, if you wanted, the ripple part. You could pretend it was just a water bug, say, disturbing the surface. That was what she did: chose to feel the sting and the hug as one thing, with no ripples. Touched her barely pregnant belly as if to take a pulse—just checking, everything would be okay, she would make it okay. He's really a good man, just under a lot of stress, that's all. The women always said things like that but in her case, she believed it was true. She was an artist, a college graduate, the daughter of a high school principal. She was twenty-six years old.

Her name was Mollie, and she was not the sort of woman whose husband hit her.

Though the hot puffy welt rising across her cheek suggested otherwise.

OF COURSE NO ONE COULD KNOW, another thing the women always say, but doubly true in Mollie's case, because it was a small town, and she used to work at the organic food store, and she didn't shave her legs, and she used natural remedies for poison ivy and teething and earaches, and she made her own bread, and she recycled everything, and lived, she hoped, in a way that did not harm the earth, because she loved the earth and her own life and her children, and she still loved him, even though he said things like, your breasts are wrecked from all the nursing.

HIS NAME WAS GIL, and the irony of his profession did not escape her. He was a physical therapist. He worked for a fitness center, which was where they met. She was taking a yoga class there. She liked him, the dark, brooding type. Back then, trouble was interesting. Now she wished she had picked someone sunny, self-assured, joyful, the way she used to be, studying aromatherapy, painting and sculpting until three or four in the morning, cooking elaborate vegetarian casseroles. He had fallen in love with her, he said, because she was the first happy person he had ever seen up close.

WERE THERE SIGNS? She was a smart girl. Had she seen signs? Some warning when they were dating? A push, a shove? Isn't that

how the experts say it always starts? A belittling comment, pos-
sessiveness, isolation from friends.

She shook her head, ice pack on her cheek, children in front of
the TV, again.

Yes, okay. There were signs.

SHE FOUND THE MOST AMAZING THINGS coming out of her mouth:
Just don't hit me in front of the children. Just don't hit my face,
Isabel's coming over tomorrow. Just don't hit my stomach, you'll
hurt the baby. Once she even put Zach to bed, then came back to
the kitchen to get punched, like an obedient child who needed a
spanking. But she didn't even believe in spanking. She never hit
her children. He didn't hit them either. If he had, she would have
stabbed him with a paring knife.

SHE WAS AFRAID. Not of being hit, but of being left. She used to
believe in God. She used to believe in being honest with herself, her
friends, her parents. Now she believed in pretending. If he left—she
was pregnant now, with a third child—what could she do? They
had to stay together, at least until she figured something out. She
tried to think of ways she could make some money, just in case. For
a while she worked the drive-thru at Taco Bell. It was awful. She
was an artist, she wanted to make beautiful things, like the pots she
had made in her ceramics class, the ones he had thrown at her one
afternoon while the babies napped, the ones whose pieces she had
collected in a grocery bag and put in the closet under the stairs. A
nice dark place—she had hidden there once, when he had come
home early, and the children were at the neighbor's. She had stayed
there, in the dark, knowing he'd think they had all gone out
somewhere. He talked to himself then, and he didn't sound like a

twenty-eight-year-old physical therapist with soft hands and a formerly open heart. She heard a word here and there. Something about the house, and some praying sounds. She crouched in the darkness, breathing mothballs and cat urine and clay dust from her broken pots. She was crying now, which she hadn't permitted herself to do very much. She could hear him on the other side of the door, and knew what would happen if he found her.

THE FIRST TIME HAD BEEN A FIGHT over a computer she bought at a yard sale. She wanted it for Zach; Joshua wasn't born yet. It was a piece of crap, Gil said. It was outdated, ten years old, new software wouldn't even run on it. Twenty-five dollars down the drain, and the electric bill due that week. She had yelled back. Defended her dumb choice. She was trying to see it from his point of view now, trying to stand in the kitchen where he had stood, right in that spot where the vinyl flooring was cracked and peeling. She could see the grime around the faucet, the breakfast dishes still in the sink, the blob of strawberry jam on the counter, her own anger, the hand drawn back, away from her, then, unbelievably, toward her. To make everything stop, he had said later, weeping. Just to make things stop.

After that, there were other reasons. No shortage of reasons. The messy house. The crying children. The money troubles. The outgrown clothes. The unplanned pregnancies. The way she looked at the baby. The way she looked at Zach. The way she talked to the neighbor. The way she talked on the phone. It was the Goodwill furniture, the rips in the cushions of the plaid couch, the crumbling dirty yellow foam rubber. It was the college loans, store-brand macaroni and cheese for dinner, bald tires on the '86 Tercel, porch steps that needed fixing but the goddamned landlord who wouldn't. It was the way she looked or didn't look, the stupid way she spent the money he earned, the lack of gratitude. It was his father, for whom nothing was ever good enough. It was her mother, who had spoiled her rotten before dropping dead and leaving them not so much as a single cent. It was her selfish step-father, who had the money and wouldn't give them so much as a single cent. It was the foolish ideas she had about selling her pots, her paintings, her jewelry, her plant hangers, her herbs, her home-made candles, her poems, her weaving, her collages, her children's books, her sculptures, her whatever it was this week.

It used to be everyone else he was angry with. Now it was her. She didn't know when that shift occurred. She had been out of the room for that one.

THERE WAS THIS NATIVE AMERICAN MAN at the farmers' market every Saturday. Mollie dreamed that Gil went to him for healing. The market was six blocks from their house. She walked there, quite pregnant now, the other two children stacked in the stroller, squabbling, sticky, hot. She bought bunches of basil to make pesto because Gil hated her breath when she ate garlic and wouldn't try to have sex with her. She bought bouquets of flowers she couldn't afford. She bought homemade preserves from an old lady whose husband had died during the winter, but who still set up a folding chair for him. Mollie saw people she knew, and smiled, shining and full—pregnancy made her especially beautiful, even he said that. She had two boys, four-year-old Zach and two-year-old Joshua, and she was hoping for a girl. But she never said so. What good would it do? She remembered the Eliot poem from her freshman English class: "I said to my soul, be still, and wait without hope/ For hope would be hope for the wrong thing." That was what she was doing. Being still. Waiting without hope. It wasn't, she felt, as desperate as it sounded.

The medicine man from her dream was actually Mexican, or part Mexican anyway. His name turned out to be Ford. She didn't know if that was his last name or his first name. In her dream, Gil went to him and Ford gave him a vial of something made with roots and oils and extracts, and when he drank it, his face changed, "morphed" Zach would say, and she could see it, the change coming over Gil, how he would be gentle again, how he would touch her with his strong warm hands and love her with his old heart that had inexplicably gone dark and cold.

FORD GAVE HER THE IDEA TO SELL HER BREAD at the farmers' market. He saw her ripping hunks off a homemade loaf for the children as she bought her weekly vegetables and flowers. "Can I have some?" He was flirting, but she didn't mind. As long as Gil wasn't there. She tore him off a piece, even though they both knew he had been kidding. He chewed, his eyes widening, a parody of a compliment. Then he shook his head more seriously. "You should sell your bread here. Jana used to, but she moved to Omaha. You'd make a killing."

She was nothing if not willing. So she applied for a permit to set up a table at the market, then spent the week baking, borrowing her neighbor's freezer to store the bread she made early in the week. On Saturday morning she stacked all the loaves in the stroller, put Joshua in the backpack carrier, and made Zach walk to the market. She set up next to Ford, who had, kindly, brought an extra table. She cut up samples of bread and put them on a ceramic plate that had been spared Gil's fury. People came to see Ford, because he was handsome and had the best vegetables, and he urged them to try Mollie's bread, and they bought up the loaves within the first hour and a half, leaving her their names—would she save a loaf for them next week?

She made ninety-six dollars that day.

She put half the cash in a savings account, gave the rest to Gil. "Not much," he said.

"Better than nothing," she said, and he nodded.

She borrowed her neighbor's car and loaded up on supplies at a wholesale store. She checked out cookbooks from the library and chose recipes for three new kinds of bread. She found a commercial mixer at an auction. The baby inside her was running out of room, kicking her aggressively and hiccupping at regular intervals. Her sons sat at the kitchen table, watching as she mixed enormous batches of dough, the dense smells of yeast and milk and butter surrounding them like love, the brown loaves emerging endlessly from the oven, things of beauty.

# lost spirits

The séances at my grandmother's house began—and ended—the summer I was twelve. My mother and I had just moved into a guest cottage on my grandparents' property in Massachusetts, after three years of living the good life, as she called it, in St. Petersburg. We left because Mother lost her job playing the piano at the Idle Hours. A fight with the owner, she said, but never elaborated. My mother was never big on details. She always talked in terms of the big picture, the general idea. My mother was the most beautiful woman in the world; she didn't need to get specific. Now she said we were in a period of transition. We were taking the summer off. I knew this meant we were broke.

It wasn't clear how long we would live in the cottage. Probably just the summer, but maybe longer. Something would work out. In the meantime, I was to entertain myself and make the best of things.

We had lived with my grandparents a week when Teddy, my grandmother, made her announcement. "Philip," she said to me,

"Jane and Eva are coming over tonight for a séance. Help me set up the dining room, would you?"

Séances, as far as I knew, were for sixth-grade girls at slumber parties. My expression must have betrayed what I was thinking. "Stop looking at me like I've lost my mind. It's Jane's idea, not mine." Jane was Teddy's younger sister, known in the family for her tireless pursuit of matrimony—she had had nine husbands. At the age of seventy-two, she was looking for number ten. Jane's interests in the occult had developed fairly recently, according to her skeptical sister.

"She began going to this spiritualist church and reading books about astral traveling," Teddy explained. We were moving the heavy dining room table to one side and setting up a card table in the middle of the room. Jane and two friends of hers, including Eva, the medium who presided over the séances, had been holding their meetings every Friday night at Jane's house. They had made so much noise the neighbors complained.

"Noise?" I asked. "What sort of—noise?"

"Who knows? Banging and thumping, I suppose. Jane lives in a duplex; the walls are made of Kleenex. I told her she could come out here if she wanted. She so looks forward to her Friday evenings."

"Are you going to the séance, Teddy?"

"I said I'd sit in. They're missing their third party—she's off at some parapsychology school for the summer. Do you want to join us, Philip? The more the merrier, I'm sure."

I said yes before giving it much thought. I had nothing else to do, after all, except read and ride my bike and hang around Hamilton, my grandfather, while he gardened or sat on the porch, smoking cigars and "staying out of the old woman's way," as he put it. Which seemed like a good idea, considering the debris that often covered Teddy's kitchen floor the morning after one of their fights—silverware and cork coasters and plastic bowls and anything else my grandmother could throw at him without doing any real damage. I never knew what Ham did to provoke Teddy on such a regular basis, but I suppose his long periods of reticence, broken only by an occasional drinking binge or a practical joke at her expense, had taken their toll over the years.

Mother and I ate our meals in the cottage, which sat at the edge of a small pond where my grandfather kept his ducks. That night, over Chinese meatballs, I told my mother about the séances. She didn't look too surprised.

"Jane always was quite a character," she said.

"So do you think they really contact ghosts?"

My mother looked at me thoughtfully as she licked soy sauce from her silk kimono sleeve, which she dipped inadvertently into almost every evening meal. "I suppose anything's possible," she said, and put another meatball in her mouth.

At a quarter till eight that evening I walked up to the house, a short distance in daylight but one that I knew would lengthen dramatically in the dark. For a moment I felt the full absurdity of my position. What other twelve-year-old boy was, in the height of summer, going to a séance at his grandmother's? Standing outside the strange old house, with its haphazard additions poking out from all sides, I felt briefly but deeply sorry for myself. What a stupid life I led, and how powerless I was to change it. I sighed and went to greet the old women.

Jane was wearing a pink and orange muumuu. Her sixth husband, the accountant, had bought it for her in Honolulu, the night he choked to death. She was hoping to contact him tonight, and thought the muumuu might help. She gave me an energetic hug, then stepped back and with a graceful sweep of her arm introduced the large woman sitting on the couch as Eva Martinelli, the medium.

Eva kept her blue eyes opened very wide, as if she might miss something if she blinked; this, in combination with the way her white hair was brushed straight back from her pale broad forehead, made her look like a woman standing in a wind tunnel.

Teddy had told me that Eva had had cancer years ago, and the treatments left her without eyebrows or eyelashes—they never grew back. (Neither did the half a lung the surgeons removed.) Instead of real eyebrows, there were two brown penciled arches like upside-down U's above her eyes. She wheezed as she breathed, reminding me of an asthmatic cat we once had.

"So nice to meet you, Philip. I always welcome children to our gatherings; they have a unique psychic presence."

I didn't know what to say to that. We all looked around at each other, and then Jane said, "Well! Shall we go in?" and we filed, Indian style, into the dining room, which candlelight had transformed into an unfamiliar place full of jittery shadows and black corners.

As we all sat around the card table, our hands resting lightly on its surface, the tips of our left pinky fingers resting on the fingernail of the pinky to our left, I began to wonder about the dead people who might be out there, looking for me.

I NEVER KNEW MY FATHER. When my mother became pregnant with me, she was a twenty-year-old secretary who spent her Friday and Saturday nights singing in the cocktail lounge of the Poughkeepsie Holiday Inn. Teddy had a picture of her from that time hanging in the living room. She looked like a fresh-faced model for *Seventeen* magazine—a shining all-American girl with a blond beehive and a small turned-up nose, a smile straight out of a toothpaste ad, and almost disconcertingly light green eyes. She hoped to land a gig in a New York City club as a jazz singer, and much of her time in those days was spent trying to make connections. My father was one of those connections: a bartender at a club in the Village who, shortly after impregnating my mother, was drafted into the army. At least, this was the story she had always told me.

"Ernie and I weren't really all that close," she confided to me on more than one occasion. "Not that I slept around or anything. Though people certainly did in those days. It was 1969, after all. The summer of love."

My mother never sounded bitter during these discussions. She never seemed curious about my father's fate, had apparently never bothered to follow up on him at all. I assumed he was missing in action, or dead, or back home in the States somewhere with his real family. I resigned myself to the fact that I would never know him.

At least until the night of the first séance.

It occurred to me, while we were sitting in the dark room, waiting for the spirits to join us, that if my father were dead, as I often told my friends, then he might want to contact me. I had never had a conversation with my father before. What would I say to him?

Eva told us to close our eyes. She murmured some sort of prayer, then she began making *ommm* sounds, long rumbling humming sounds, like something emanating from the middle of the earth. My palms were sweating, but I couldn't pick them up off the table, especially now—the table had begun to move.

We opened our eyes. I looked for possible tricks. Maybe this was all a game. Maybe the old ladies were trying to fool me. But Teddy looked as surprised as I felt, and as far as I could tell Jane and Eva couldn't possibly be moving the table by themselves. No—there was something moving underneath our hands, an energy like electricity or heat, something you could feel but not see. The table shook back and forth, its spindly legs tapping the floor lightly at first, then more insistently.

"Spirit," Eva rumbled. "If you are a good spirit, you are welcome to our gathering. If you are evil, then go home!" The table continued to vibrate, as steadily as one of those hotel room beds that you stick a quarter in.

"Spirit, we will ask you questions so that you may identify

yourself. If the answer is yes, then stop moving the table. If the answer is no, continue to move. Do you understand?"

The table stopped as abruptly as if it had been unplugged. Yes. It understood. The vibrations resumed.

"Good!" Eva smiled triumphantly. "Now. Spirit. We are hoping to contact Jack Altman. Jack Altman, husband of Jane, who is here with us tonight." A dramatic pause while Eva struggled for air. "Is this Jack?" The table continued its shaking.

"No, it's not Jack," Jane said sadly.

"Spirit, is Jack there?"

The table hesitated slightly, as if whoever was moving it around had paused for a moment to look over his shoulder. Then it resumed, steady, back and forth. My mouth felt completely dry. All the moisture in my body had flooded to my palms and armpits.

"Okay, Spirit," Eva said. "Is there someone here you would like to talk to?"

The table stopped. We lurched forward.

"Ah! My! All right, Spirit, is it Jane you wish to speak to?" The table shook. "Is it Theodora? Teddy? Do you wish to speak to Teddy?" My grandmother's eyes narrowed in concentration. But the table moved on, like a train clicking steadily toward its destination. "Do you wish to speak to me, Spirit?" No, no, no, the table shook impatiently. Eva smiled at me as if I had done something particularly precocious, her blue eyes wider than ever. "Ahhh … it's Teddy's Philip, then? Do you wish to speak to—"

And just as the table came to its inevitable pitching halt, a banging noise filled the room. It seemed to come from everywhere. The floor thudded with it. We all sprang to our feet, releasing our fingertips from the table and, I guessed, releasing the spirit who had come for me.

BANG! BANG!

"What on earth?" Jane exclaimed.

Eva had started to pray, her hands held outward, palms up, eyes closed. Teddy listened to the banging for a second and then tore out of the room, heading for the cellar and yelling her husband's name.

Of course. It was Hamilton down there, banging on the cellar ceiling with a broom handle or his walking stick. I laughed out loud, the nervousness that had been gathering for the last hour escaping in one big guffaw. My grandfather, who usually went to bed at seven-thirty, had managed to stay up long enough—and wait for just the right moment—to play his prank. I could hear him coughing and chortling as he slowly climbed the stairs to his room. My grandmother apologized, but the good-natured Eva said not to worry, spirits were not so easily deterred as that.

This time the table started moving as soon as our hands touched the surface. Eva verified that this was the same spirit as before, then turned to me and asked, "Any ideas, Philip?"

I could feel Teddy looking at me. I kept my eyes on the table. For a moment, I couldn't get any words out. When I spoke, my voice was thin with embarrassment. "Is it—is it my father? Is it Ernie?" I held my breath, but the table kept shaking.

"No," Eva sighed. "No, it's not Ernie. Teddy? Any ideas?"

Teddy proceeded to reel off six or seven names, but I was trying to hide my disappointment and didn't hear. The table finally stopped when she mentioned Oscar, somebody's half-brother from two generations ago. Oscar, Teddy explained, had died at thirteen or fourteen in a farming accident.

Eva spoke in a loud voice again. "Oscar dear, do you have a message for Philip?" The table hesitated, then kept going. Eva nodded and looked at me knowingly. "Oscar was probably attracted to you because you are young, Philip, and living near his home on earth." She wheezed for a moment, rocking to Oscar's rhythm, then continued. "Oscar, did you come to Philip because you are lonely?" The table halted in a definite yes. "Everyone, close your eyes, and let us send this poor spirit home." We all closed our eyes, but I opened mine immediately. I wanted to see exactly what was going on.

"Oscar," Eva breathed. "Look around you. Do you see a white light, Oscar? A very bright, white light?" In the dining room's dim light, Eva's broad forehead was the color of the moon. Again, the table hesitated slightly, but then stopped, all at once, as if to say Yes! There it is!

"Good. Now, I want you to listen carefully. You are in a strange place now, but if you go to the white light you will be home." Her voice became louder and her breathing more labored with every sentence. "Go to the white light and you will find peace! You will find your loved ones! Do you understand?" The table shuddered to a halt, moved again. "Will you go to the white light?" Eva was practically shouting now, and gulping air between words. The table stopped more emphatically this time. "Go home now, Oscar," Eva gasped. The table settled down gradually, and then was still.

"That's enough for one night," Eva said, exhausted.

She slowly opened her eyes. Her gaze was so steady I couldn't have looked away if I tried. "Oscar was lost," she said quietly. "He didn't know he had passed, you see. He's been wandering around all these years, poor soul ... thinking he's still with us. This happens sometimes, when the passing is sudden and unexpected."

I was dumbfounded. For a moment I forgot about my father. "You mean—you're telling me that this kid got run over by a tractor and didn't know he was dead?" I had this image of a mangled boy hanging around the cottage, trying to get my attention. Had I been brushing him aside without realizing it? Had he been tapping my shoulder, pulling on my sleeve with his bloody hands, sitting with my mother and me at our little table as we played Crazy Eights, pleading with us to deal him in? Did he think we were just ignoring him?

"A very difficult situation," Eva was saying. "It happens all the time, I'm afraid." Eva hoisted herself up with great effort, and declined my grandmother's invitation for coffee. She was tired, she said; worn out from Oscar's sorrow.

Teddy said she wanted to get some air, and walked me to the

cottage. Neither of us mentioned that I might be spooked, but I was.

"So, Teddy. Do you—do you think we really, you know, contacted a ghost?"

"I don't know, Philip. Certainly something was happening in that room. Now, there are other explanations besides spirits."

"Like what?"

"Well, maybe we all have some, I don't know, energy strong enough to cause tables to move. Maybe we have capabilities that we aren't even aware of. So that when we sit in a room and concentrate, maybe we can make these marvelous things happen. We can form, together, another ... presence." She looked down at me—we had reached the cottage now—and smiled. "Did it scare you, darling? If it did, don't feel you have to come back next week."

"I'll come back, Teddy," I said. She didn't mention my father, and I was glad.

My mother was sitting at the table with a green mud pack on her face, her shampooed hair in a towel, her kimono exchanged for a pink nightgown. Her stationery lay on the formica table next to a chipped saucer with toast crumbs on it. She had been writing letters to her contacts. In the last two weeks, five such letters had been "returned to sender, addressee unknown." For a moment I felt that our situation was hopeless.

"Hello there. Did you talk to anybody from the Other Side?" The green mask made her teeth look yellow.

"You look like the Bride of Frankenstein."

"You know Friday night is mud-pack night. Sit down here for a minute and be nice. Tell me about your evening."

I looked at her for a moment, then relented. The truth is, I rarely behaved badly with my mother. The older I got, the more fragile she seemed to me, and the more in need of my protection. But the séance had put me out of sorts. I kept thinking about Oscar, and all the other lost spirits that must be out there, trying to make contact with somebody—anybody. I kept thinking about what an awful life it would be, the life of a ghost, always hanging around waiting for something to happen. It would be like being twelve forever.

I told my mother about the moving table and about Hamilton banging on the basement ceiling. That made her laugh. I didn't tell her about Oscar, though, or about my hoping to contact my father. But as she peeled the mud mask off her face, I asked her who we knew that was dead.

"Well, let's see. Dead people. What a strange question." She stood at the kitchen sink and splashed water on her pink face, then patted it dry with a ratty dishtowel. "Okay, well, there was that little boy who lived next door to us in New Jersey, do you remember him?"

"Charlie Vanderhouten? The kid who got hit by the ice cream truck?"

"Poor little Charlie."

"But Mom, Charlie didn't actually die. He was in the hospital for about a hundred years, but he lived through it. Don't you remember the big welcome home party when he finally got out? They hired that magician who drank all of Mr. Vanderhouten's homemade beer, and threw up into his magic hat, and—"

"What a memory you have, Philip. Okay, so forget Charlie. Charlie's still among the living. My, this is a morbid conversation."

"What about my father?"

"Your ... father? Oh, honey, I doubt very much that Ernie is dead."

"He was in the war, wasn't he? A lot of people got killed, didn't they?" I realized as I spoke that I had begun counting on my father's death. If he wasn't dead, how was I ever going to talk to him?

"Yes, a lot of people died in the war. That's true. But somehow I just can't picture Ernie getting killed. I just can't see it happening. He was more the shoot-off-your-big-toe-and-get-discharged type."

"But you don't know for sure. He might be dead. He might not. You don't know."

"Philip, this obsession with your father. I understand that it's perfectly normal—"

"You don't know for sure if he's dead or alive."

She looked at me, her eyes more lucid than I had ever seen them, the usual playful naiveté gone. My heart raced. I was looking at a different person. I wondered if she was possessed, if I had unknowingly brought home some weird spirit who had taken over her body. This was not the mother I knew. This woman was an adult, and she scared me.

"You don't know for sure," I repeated, whispering this time.

"Yes, Philip," she finally said, her voice calm and clear. "I do know. Your father is alive."

MY MOTHER HAD LIED TO ME. Ernie Stevens was not just a fling to her. He was, she admitted, the love of her life. When she told him she was pregnant, he left her. He ran away. He didn't get drafted. He never served in the military. He flunked his army physical months before he even met my mother. He flunked because of his lousy feet, which, by the way, he passed on to me.

"Ernie and I were talking about getting married. Then I got pregnant, and suddenly he didn't want to talk marriage anymore. 'This is going too fast,' he said. 'This is too heavy.' 'How do you think it feels for me?' I asked him. But he didn't have an answer for that. Those were selfish days, Philip. Don't believe what else people might tell you about the summer of love. Everybody was just out for themselves. Ernie was out for himself. I was out for myself. But I was also out for you."

I nodded. I felt so stupid. All those years, I had believed her lost-in-the-war story. What choice did I have?

"I know how you must feel, Philip. But think of me, too. I lost Ernie. I was alone in the world. Then you were born, and I wasn't alone anymore. It didn't matter anymore how you got here. You were here. That's all that mattered."

"I don't want to talk about this anymore," I said, and went to my room.

In bed I listened to the bullfrogs and the crickets, and thought about my mother's lie. She had told me that the last she heard, Ernie was out west somewhere. Portland, or Eugene. He was married, had kids, was running his own restaurant. I had no desire to see him, ever. But it was the first time in my whole life that I had gone to bed knowing for a fact that my father existed someplace, and I felt strange, lightheaded almost, as if I were hovering over myself, looking down, floating, separate from my body.

"I miss St. Petersburg," my mother said from her bedroom. The cottage was so small that we often had conversations like this, from different rooms. "Maybe we could move back there. Would you like that, Philip?"

"Sure," I said. I didn't care where we lived at the moment. We could move to Russia, as far as I was concerned. We could move to Tanzania.

"Maybe this will just turn out to be our summer vacation, and not a transition period after all."

"Maybe."

"In the meantime, we just need to make the best of things, that's all. We just need to ..." Her voice drifted off, and there was a brief, heavy silence. "Don't be mad at me, sweetheart. I couldn't bear it if you were mad at me."

"I'm not mad, Mom."

But we both knew the truth.


IN THE DAYS AND WEEKS THAT FOLLOWED, I spent a lot of time with Ham. We didn't have to talk just for the sake of talking, and he was the only person I could be with in that way. He had no words of wisdom for me, just his solid presence as he weeded his gardens, kneeling on one knee like a man about to propose marriage. He always wore a tattered canvas hat to protect the bald spot on his head from the sun. Beneath the hat his light blue eyes surveyed his property with bemusement, as if he didn't quite know how he had arrived in such a place. His work clothes had a familiar sweaty smell, and his hands were old and red, weathered like his face. I loved to watch his hands at work. He put his fingers right into the dirt and pulled the weeds up by their roots. He didn't mind getting dirt under his fingernails. He plunged right in.

EVERY FRIDAY NIGHT THAT SUMMER, we had a séance. It seemed as if every member of my extended family who had died within the last two hundred years paid a visit to our table. They never had any messages for us, and I came to the conclusion that spirits, like regular people, really didn't have anything very important to say. They just wanted some attention.

My mother and I didn't discuss Ernie anymore. I did my best not to think about him, or about my mother's past. She did her best to pretend our conversation had never happened. She was dating a new man now, Christopher Jenkins, a band teacher at the local high school. He was a tall skinny man with serious eyes that examined my mother's every movement from behind round wire-rim glasses. I had seen this look in my mother's dates before. Frankly, it made me a little nauseated. But my mother seemed happy with this Jenkins character, so I tried to behave well around him. I don't think he noticed one way or the other, though. He was concentrating too hard on developing x-ray vision that would pierce the silk of my mother's kimono, or the pale paisleys of her faded sundress.

IN LATE JULY, DURING OUR LAST SÉANCE, we contacted Teddy's father. He was the only spirit who came with a message, but Teddy didn't want to hear it. "You deserted us," she hissed. "You drank up all the money. Mother had to work eighteen hours a day in the pharmacy. We were a disgrace. I don't want any messages from you." But Teddy's father wouldn't leave the table.

"He's very persistent," Eva said. "I think you should listen."

Jane, who was younger and less bitter than Teddy, persuaded her to take their father's message.

We turned on the lights. Eva instructed us to write the letters of the alphabet on small pieces of paper. We placed them along the edge of the oval dining room table. We wrote Yes and No and the numbers 0 to 9 and arranged them according to Eva's directions. We were all excited. We'd seen the vibrating-table trick over and over; this promised to be something new.

Eva took a wineglass from the china cabinet and put it on the table, upside down. She and Teddy rested their fingertips lightly upon the base of the glass. And then a startling thing happened. Right away, the glass moved. It glided over the table magically. It circled the letters like a graceful skater, and stopped precisely in front of the letter it wanted. Jane sat poised with a pencil and a pad like a stenographer as Eva called out the letters. "I!"—and around they went, two old ladies chasing after a speeding wine glass so their fingers wouldn't slip off. "A! ... M! ..."

"I am," Jane translated expectantly.

"S! ... O! ... S! ... O!" Eva clutched her heaving chest and gasped for breath.

"So-so?" Jane wondered aloud.

"It's still going," I told her.

"R!" the medium wheezed. "And R again! And Y!" The glass stopped. Eva was bent over, hands on her knees, gulping air like a dog hanging outside a car window.

"I ... am ... so ... sorry," Jane read proudly.

Teddy and Jane looked at each other for a moment before

Teddy shook her head and left the room. I could hear her in the kitchen, running the water and putting dishes away with a clatter.

"That's enough for tonight," Eva said, blowing her nose into an enormous hanky. She whispered a prayer between heavy sighs and wheezes. We collected the little pieces of paper and threw them away, then folded up the card table. I noticed, when I said good night to Teddy, that she had tears in her eyes.

I wondered, as I walked to the cottage alone, if what moved her about the message was the same thing that moved me. What moved me was that "so." I am *so* sorry. A sincere spirit, I thought. A spirit who knows that sometimes it takes a little extra effort to get your message across really effectively. I knew it was effective, because the next day Teddy decided she was done with the séance business, and she told Jane and Eva that they could go to someone else's house from now on.

In the days that followed, I kept thinking about Teddy's father. I couldn't get him out of my mind. I even told my mother about him.

"He should've spoken up while he was still alive," Mother said. "He should have said something."

I nodded. We were sitting outside in two deck chairs, Teddy's card table between us, playing gin rummy. Already the air felt like late summer; the pond smelled like dead leaves, and the water looked dark and cold.

My mother had that focused look she got when she was about to beat me at cards. I tried to distract her. "Where's that band teacher, anyway? Ol' Mr. Jenkins? Haven't seem him around here lately."

She just smiled and laid out her hand. "Gin," she said.


A COUPLE OF WEEKS LATER MOTHER GOT A PHONE CALL from her old boss at the Idle Hours, wondering if she wanted her job back.

The girl who had replaced my mother was a tramp, he said; she'd gotten pregnant and run off. He needed someone he could rely on. I was happy when my mother gave me the news. Of all the places we had lived, St. Petersburg felt like home to me. We decided to stay in Massachusetts until the end of August. The Idle Hours wanted her back after Labor Day; we would move in time for the new school year.

That afternoon I was hanging around Teddy's kitchen while she rolled out biscuit dough for dinner. Now that I knew we were leaving for sure, I was beginning to feel nostalgic about our summer together, even about the séances. I remembered meeting Eva for the first time, and how strange she seemed to me. After a few Fridays, though, she didn't seem strange at all. She just seemed like Eva. I wondered about the last séance, and about the wineglass under Teddy's fingertips. Nobody had said a word about the séances since. But the time seemed right to ask my grandmother about it now.

"Teddy, what did it feel like, when that wineglass was going around the table?" I was careful not to mention her father.

She stopped rolling the dough and looked at me over her glasses. "Well, Philip, it felt very strange."

"Were your fingers just barely touching the glass, or—"

"Just barely touching."

"So you didn't—you don't think Eva—"

"I don't know. Maybe subconsciously, maybe we helped it along without meaning to, you know. But the glass was moving so fast, I could barely keep my fingertips on it, and Eva of course could hardly keep up with it. So I don't think we were moving it. There are always other explanations, of course." Teddy's voice faded a little. "Other possibilities."

"The message was nice, I thought." I was moving into dangerous territory, I knew. But I kept going. "I thought the 'so' was kind of nice. Not just, I'm sorry, but—I am so sorry."

She cut some biscuits out with the open end of an orange juice can, and laid them in careful rows on the cookie sheets. "Yes. I suppose. I suppose it's better than nothing."

We stood in the kitchen like this for a few moments, thinking. Then she took two big oatmeal cookies from the jar and said, "Take one to Ham."

I found my grandfather kneeling on one knee, weeding his garden. I looked around the yard at all his careful work, the shrubberies and the beds of flowers and rhododendron and all the trees he had planted long ago that were now so tall I could hardly see the tops of them. It was pleasant there, with the late afternoon light shining on everything, a light that was clear and clean and almost tangibly soft. Enough time had passed now since the last séance that I had almost forgotten about all the spirits wandering around the world. I wasn't so worried anymore that they were trying to catch my attention, that they were hanging around the cottage watching TV, or poking around our kitchen, looking for something to eat. I was able to look at Ham's yard without straining to see them, the souls of unhappy dead people waving at me from the tall trees. It was nice just to look at the world again, and to see just the world looking back.

I handed a cookie to my grandfather. "So you all are going back down to Florida now," he said.

"Yup. I'll miss you, Ham."

He nodded and began weeding again. "You know, anytime you need a place to stay, that cottage is always available. We've kept it up for your mother over the years. We'll keep it up for you." His blue eyes peered up at me from beneath the tattered canvas hat.

"I'll keep that in mind."

He smiled at me, as if we shared a secret. Then he gestured toward the flower bed, and I knelt down next to him and plunged my hands into the soft, dark earth.

# green beans

I. Annie

Tents in the yard. Four of them. People sleeping off hangovers and whatever else from last night's party. It's the country, gravel roads where every few years a high school kid rolls his pickup and gets tossed out the windshield into a field, his body hitting so hard that it makes an indentation in the earth before bouncing a few more times and, finally, stopping. Idiots—in such a hurry to get into that ground. I know about the chopped-up grass and dirt and the limbs twisted at odd angles and the necks broken like dry sticks, because the man I live with happens to be the county coroner, so he pronounces these deaths. Pronounces, like a difficult word, one you've never seen before. Or maybe you've seen it but can't remember how to say it. *Ignominy* is like that, for me.

I'm in the garden early because I was in bed early. I'm twenty-six years old and I have already quit drinking. Plus, it'll be too hot later. Plus, I've got a bumper crop of green beans, and if I don't pick a basketful now, to give away to these friends and friends of friends as they pile into their cars and head back to town after brunch, the beans will rot. Right now they dangle in the shade of the leaves, damp with dew, their cool slenderness a pleasure. I pluck the beans and wonder where Doc spent the night. He never came to bed so maybe he passed out in the hammock or else drowned in the pond out back during a midnight swim, and I'll have to go fish out his body when I'm done bringing in these beans.

I've lived here since I was eighteen, when Doc pulled me from my flipped-over Honda. I was on my way somewhere else, driving straight through, but he convinced me to stay with him for a while. The while turned into longer than I meant. Then it got hard to leave.

I carry the basket to the house, set it on the big oak table in the kitchen. I crack a dozen eggs into a ceramic bowl, watching out the window for signs of life. I grate cheese, chop scallions, slice mushrooms, heat up a huge iron skillet and drop in a half-stick of butter. Last week I got my hair cut too short. Now it sticks up all over my head like dandelion fuzz. I rinse my hands and run them through the spiky ends.

What's the one thing that matters? my friend Judy asked me once, long distance from Maine. I was sitting in the wicker rocker on the front porch, talking to Judy on the portable phone and looking out over the pasture that stretches to the creek, and at the skinny line of road that splits the hill to the north of us like parted hair. Tell me the one thing, she said. The view's not bad, I said. And there's Doc. I thought about waiting for him to come home at night, and how I'm always glad to see him. Doesn't that count for something? I asked her. After eight years, doesn't that count?

Hmm, she said.

I hear the sound of laughing through the screen door, and I look out at the blue and grey tents and see Doc stumbling out of the one that's pitched furthest from the house. Then I see the girl who's with him. Shelli? Sherri? I never heard her name right. But I remember her from the party; she helped me with the potato salad. She's wearing a bikini top and a pair of white cutoffs. I'm trying to recall the string of moments that has brought me to this one: a skillet of eggs bubbling on the stove, a basket of green beans sitting on the table I refinished last winter, a man walking into the house and not even bothering to pretend, as if this is what I'm for.

Morning, the girl says as she walks through my kitchen on the way to the bathroom. Polite, not ironic. This girl, greeting me like an obedient child. As if I'm the mother, not the wife.

Of course, I'm not the wife. Or the mother. Or anything.

Doc goes upstairs for his cigarettes and I'm gone before he comes back down, gone before the omelette is cooked through in the center, gone before the girl even towels off from her shower. On the passenger seat next to me is Doc's wallet and the basket of beans, which I'll eat for my breakfast and lunch, too. I'll toss the ends out the open window. I don't want to stop too much. I want to make good time. The rear tires kick back gravel and sand and I'm taking the hills fast, seat belt on, radio blaring a song whose words I used to know. It's all coming back to me, though. By the time I reach the highway, I'm singing right along.


II. Karen


I'M ON THE LIST. The list of casserole women. I've been on it for years, it's a thing the women at church do, and I've taken to church now like a sponge trying to fill up all those empty porous holes. Oh, yes, I'm keeping busy, I tell my mother when she calls. This whole thing has been hardest on her, so I talk about my job at the county clerk's office and I talk about deacons, board of trustees, coffee hour, flower committee, church growth committee, casseroles, and she, a good churchwoman, presses her lips together (I can hear her doing it, it's in the shape of the words that come out right after) and sighs and says, Well, Karen, I just hope you're all right.

I thought by now I'd be chauffeuring kids around in my minivan, wearing stretch pants and hastily applied lipstick, and I wanted to be that person, not this one who tries to empty the hours from her days like someone bailing water from a sinking boat— they just keep coming. I try to focus on the task before me. These days, this is my true religion: the task before me. At night, a sleeping pill (Halcyon—isn't that lovely?). During the day, double lattes, aerobics classes, and the task before me. I keep a list, on a clipboard. I'm like a coach or a stage manager. I should wear a visor and a whistle around my neck. Running the show. *You're such an inspiration, how do you do it?*

You've heard of the amputee. Well, you know what? Pull out your insides, and you feel the same phantom twitch. But no—the task. Pull skin from chicken. Trim beans. Measure rice. I don't even need to look at the recipe anymore, the recipe I wrote for the *Women's Fellowship Cookbook*: Karen Leonard's Chicken, Rice, and Green Bean Deluxe Casserole. No spices or onions or garlic because they get into the breast milk and distress the tiny digestive systems of the newborn babies. I make a signature heart-shaped cake with frosting—blue or pink, depending. Load it all up into these two wooden crates I keep just for casserole duty. Now I don't even have to call over my shoulder, Just going to drop this meal off at the Clarkses' (or Noonans' or Lippincotts'). I just slam the door, load the food into the trunk, and start the car. Sometimes I hum. I make myself hum. It's a good trick for the don't-think-about-it things. I just hmmm right over them, and I hmmm my way through the new mother's front door and into her kitchen, and I hmmm over the living rooms scattered with baby gifts and baby things and somewhere, on someone's tidy smug lap, a baby. I hmmm right over the offers to hold the baby, and I hmmm over the new-baby smell that I know will be on me anyway when I get back into my car, and I hmmm a promise to myself: one little glass of wine when you get home.

What would that church do without you? the grandmothers and fathers and mothers say.

I smile, laugh. Congratulations! Good luck! Get some sleep! I hmmm right out the door, where there's no sign of Jesus or my husband anywhere.

You could adopt, people used to say. People who have made their own babies, grown them inside their own bodies, fed them with their own milk. At church potlucks they wipe their children's mouths with napkins, look brightly at you and say, You could always adopt.

They don't know quite what to say, once your husband leaves. One task, this task: Drive home. Call Pastor Daniel. Get my name off the goddamned list.

## III. Emma

IT IS TRUE THAT I PREPARED GREEN BEANS just hours before my death, but it is not as odd as it seems. After all, they were Blue Lake beans, on sale at the Safeway that week, and Kenny was always partial to them. In fact, Kenny won't eat any other green vegetable, except broccoli salad with Miracle Whip and vinegar and bacon bits. At least he didn't used to. I can't help but notice how he's become much more accommodating, vegetables-wise, with his second wife. But I wasn't thinking about that while I was fixing those last beans. I was just doing like always, sitting in my deck chair—the one with the fraying strips of white and blue fabric that sagged just where I did—snapping the curled-up antennae ends off the beans and tossing the too-skinny ones to Lulu. She'd eat anything, that dog, even iceberg lettuce. Her favorite dish was banana cream pie, my sister Betsy's recipe with the Nilla Wafer crust. I do miss that dog. And while I was throwing her those skinny ol' beans and watching her leap up to catch them in her mouth, I decided. Once that pile of beans was trimmed, that'd be it. Why drag on? It was a matter of weeks anyhow. Today I could fix supper, tomorrow have trouble drawing breath.

Of course, once I'd made up my mind, I started doing the beans real slowly.

The truth was, it was a beautiful day. The kind of day that makes you want to go on forever. A breeze tossing the highest branches of the pine trees, that creamy blue sky deep and rich and thick as paint, the pains in my chest and back not so bad, the deep regret of things never done laying low, the nasturtiums and zinnias in Kenny's garden standing up like they had hands on their hips, just sassy and knowing everything. And my sisters, each in their own homes, freed for a moment from the hand-wringing and carrying on that they'd become accustomed to on my behalf. I could feel them, out there, fixing their own beans maybe, or beating the hall rugs, dust lifting into the perfect air.

Oh! It made so much sense, that it would be that day. It felt like relief, and what's better than relief? Not even joy can beat it. It was like walking out of school on the last day and into sweet summer. Released! Kite from string, fish from hook! I poured myself a nice tall glass of bourbon and smoked a cigarette from my hidden stash because hell, why not? Down in the cellar I found the lime-green plastic Easter egg, the one with the yellow smiley face sticker on it, sitting in a basket with all the other eggs left over from last year's hunt, and I remembered my grandbabies and their cousins running around our yard, so sure of the treasure that awaited them. When I shook my green egg, it rattled satisfyingly back at me: enough saved pills to knock over a camel. I lined them up carefully on the aluminum arm of my deck chair.

For a moment, I felt just a twinge of sadness. Mostly I felt—well, a little like those crazy Hale-Bopp comet people, coins in their shoes in case they needed to make a phone call—all ready and set for that last journey. I ate my pills and finished my drink so they could do their work before Kenny got home. Dozed off there, in the sun, on my porch, the pot of beans at my feet, the pleasure of snapping off their comma ends still fresh on my pill-dusted fingers, my breath already slowing, my legs already numb, my hands resting on my lap, palms up, empty but waiting to be filled. I didn't leave a note and for a while I wished I had—but what was there to say? Steam until tender, add a little bacon grease? I love you? Goodbye? No! Everything had been said till we were all weary from the talking. Everything was done. The beans trimmed, the wind blown, the medicine taken, the breaths exhaled. Lulu licked my hand, twice, wondering, then stuck her snout into the pot of beans, but I was no longer there to stop her.

# the rice in question

Melanie, without fully considering the consequences, asked her husband (whose turn it was to cook), "Do you want me to put the lid on the rice?" Normally she wasn't allowed in the kitchen when he cooked, but she needed a paper towel, and there it was: rice and water boiling, with no lid. Charles crossed the kitchen in three long strides, a Vidalia onion in one hand. "I know you're supposed to put the lid on. It just started." Melanie saw what he thought was happening. But it wasn't happening. She needed a paper towel, and she saw the boiling water. Charles clapped the lid on the pot, turned the flame to low. "Sorry," Melanie said. Lightly. She used to say it the way she said it to her brothers when she was twelve: SOR-ry. But now she was practicing a lighter touch in all things. After all, life was good, wasn't it? Truly. She felt she should repay the universe for their good fortune—the baby, their health, their jobs—with a positive attitude. Then she saw Charles frown. The frown he wore when he was considering whether or not to start something. She started to turn, to take the paper towel back to the living room, when she heard him sniff.

"Did you just sniff at me?"

"I didn't sniff."

"You did. You sniffed. Look. I was just getting a paper towel, okay? Jenny spilled water on the coffee table." She looked into the family room to check on the baby, to make sure she wasn't eating something poisonous or choking, all of which was of course impossible given the lengths they had gone to childproof their house. They had even roped shut a china cabinet a month before she was born, and hadn't had the energy to open it since. When Jenny was born, her parents were forty-two, and while she provided them with the pure joy they had always hoped for, she also opened up a whole new set of territories to negotiate. Sometimes Melanie wondered if God had been trying to tell them something during all those years of tests and hormone shots and in-vitro fertilizations and money, money, money thrown out a huge gaping window with an insatiable sucking windy appetite. But Jenny was the best thing in their lives. They loved her deeply, passionately, beyond what they had thought possible. Their love for her had deepened their love for each other. At least on the good days.

"You're sure that's all you were doing?" Charles asked.

Melanie stood in the arched doorway of their newly renovated kitchen, studying the charcoal-grey Corian countertops, the tile floors, the copper pans hanging over the island. She looked at her husband. His bald head. She liked him bald; it made his eyes bluer, somehow, larger. But at moments like these, all she saw was the way the track lighting bounced off the huge pink shiny dome of his forehead. "Look," she began. She hated the way the anger rising in her felt: good. "Jenny spilled some water. I came into the kitchen, where the paper towels are, as a rule, kept, and I saw the water boiling and I drew your attention to that fact and I'm sorry"—a little of the SOR-ry came through here—"if you think I was horning in on your dinner preparations because I was not. I was getting a paper towel."

She took a paper towel into the living room, where ten-month-old Jenny was patting at the puddle on the table with her pudgy hands. Melanie wiped up the spill and then sat, suddenly defeated, on the Berber carpet. She ruffled her short greying hair with her fingers; pressed fingers against her olive cheekbones; took the drooling, jabbering baby onto her lap. Melanie's leggings bagged at the knees. Her sweatshirt had spit-up stains on both shoulders. All marriages, she supposed, went through patches like this, where nothing either person said could be taken at face value. Talk of paper towels or boiling rice or empty gas tanks or new shoes or overdue library books or checking account balances all stood for something else.

Melanie pushed the button on the automatic CD rack and watched the CDs flip past. When had she stopped learning about new music, she wondered. Most of her CDs were replacements of the records she'd had as a teenager. She remembered curling up on her beanbag chair in her room, burning patchouli incense even though it gave her a headache, studying the lyrics on the back of a new album as if for a test. She'd have them memorized in two afternoons, and now when she heard old songs—Joni Mitchell's "All I Want" or Carole King's "Tapestry"—she could sing every word, even if she hadn't heard them for years. The rest of her memory these days was shot, but the part that stored song lyrics of the 1970s was still, for better or worse, intact.

Okay. So it was true. She was capable of being a bit controlling. She admitted it. It was hard to have Charles in there, in her kitchen, hers because she had designed it and did most of the cooking, and she knew that she was capable of a certain … bossiness. She couldn't stop instructing him. But how was it possible for a person to steam vegetables in a skillet? A skillet! And she couldn't stand to see him slicing pieces of cantaloupe—with a bread knife—on the cutting board she reserved for raw chicken, or opening a new jar of cumin before the old jar was used up, or using a dishtowel for a potholder. And her Calphalon! She'd spent years carefully washing her Calphalon pots and pans by hand, with a special non-abrasive scrubber. But after only two years of marriage, Charles had managed to take the finish off of all but one rarely-used single-serving wok by loading them all in the dishwasher. In terms of the big picture, there was no harm done. She told herself this, often. But did he have to put leftovers in uncovered cereal bowls, instead of using the Tupperware? Had he never heard of Saran Wrap?

She shook herself. Found the David Bowie CD she had been looking for almost without knowing it. The thing was, this time she really had just needed a paper towel. What would anyone getting a paper towel have done, upon seeing the rice and water boiling? Was it true, as she had once heard on *Oprah*, that women would rather be right than happy? And if she had never been directive in the kitchen before, would she have earned the right to casually indicate the boiling rice, to simply say—oh, do you want me to put the lid on? and the sentence would mean, simply, oh, do you want me to put the lid on?

Melanie lifted the silver disc from its plastic container and dropped it into the player. She tapped the number of the song she was looking for, the song that she and Charles had danced to at a fraternity party all those years ago. He would remember it—oh, certainly! It was her trump card. He would see exactly what she was trying to do. How she was reminding him of the way they had danced together in the days when they also smoked cigarettes and drank too much keg beer and longed for each other even though they were promised to other people. She would remind him of the days before those first marriages and divorces, before the medical tests and disappointments and surprises, before the periods of ennui and the transcendent moments of love, before the rice in question had been measured out with a coffee cup and poured into the pot. Before the water had even come to a boil.

# the trouble with you is

I had no plan. When you have no plan, your life ends up being about some guy you met. So I moved to Missouri. I had no plan, but he had one: a job painting houses with his cousin for the summer. Maybe in the fall he would go back to school. We drove the thousand miles in my car, a '79 Honda. He did most of the driving. I was reading an Erica Jong novel. I read the good parts out loud and he pulled into rest stops so we could have sex. His name was Mickey—Michael, but he went by Mickey. I'd never been outside of Pittsburgh much. I had no idea about all this land.

We found a basement apartment for eighty dollars a month. We split the rent, bought groceries together. He expected me to pay my share even though I didn't have a job yet. "You owe me seventeen cents for that English muffin." That kind of thing. The basement was cool but claustrophobic—a living room where I kept my manual typewriter on an upended plastic milk crate, a kitchen with no windows, a bedroom. We had a queen-size mattress on the floor, and his Muppets sheets. He loved Miss Piggy. The carpet was a green shag, the windows small rectangles. The couple above us played Michael Jackson's *Thriller* album over and over. The house was across from the newspaper building. I watched people's feet on the sidewalk, going to and from work. At four o'clock every day I walked across the street and bought a paper from the machine, for the classifieds. It was a small college town. Employment opportunities did not abound. I was twenty-one, had worked since I was fourteen. I liked to work. I liked making my own money. I had not gone to college but maybe I would, some-day. That might be a plan. While Mickey was out painting, I walked to the public library where I read for hours. I typed up my resumé and dropped it off at a few places. At night Mickey came home with paint flecks on his sunburned face, his ears, every-where. He smelled of turpentine. Mickey had thin skin. I mean that physically—he had a blond pageboy and fierce blue eyes and a wide mouth like a cut in his face and thin pale skin. You could almost see through it, the arteries and veins. He'd slip a hand under my tank top, open a beer, have a shower. I grilled sand-wiches for supper and wondered how I got there. It wasn't that I was unhappy, or happy. I just had no idea how I had ended up on that particular square foot of brown checked linoleum. I wasn't in love with Mickey, and yet I was living with him. Okay, I could understand that. I flipped a cheese sandwich. Mickey naked, out of the shower, walking up behind me, and then the sandwiches burning. We'd order pizza, eat it in bed.

MY MOTHER USED TO THROW AWAY DISHES. Clothes, too. When she got fed up with doing laundry or washing dishes she tossed the dirty stuff into a pile on the back porch. Sometimes she took the pile to the dump, or else my grandmother would come over, lips tight, and go through the whole mess, sorting clothing from

**the trouble with you is**      133

crockery. Mother would be digging in the backyard—she had plans for a fishpond and a fountain—or she was in bed with a migraine. During the migraines, my sister and I played quietly, ate spoonfuls of peanut butter for dinner. Carol was four years older and had fine straight yellow hair. We combed it out and watched it fly around her head, crackling with static electricity. We slept in the same bed even though we had our own rooms. She wrapped her thin cool arms around me like vines. After Carol left home, I went to live with my grandmother. My grandmother cleaned everything with ammonia, which is a smell that gets in your nose and never gets out.

IN JULY, I MET SOMEONE ELSE. He went to the same bar that Mickey and I went to. He played on a softball team. After their games the team drank beer there. Mickey had certain moods and one night left in the middle of a dark one. "I'm going to stay awhile," I said. "I can walk home." I had a job interview the next day and didn't plan on staying out late.

Mickey glanced at the table of softball players. He saw the bearded one with the tiny gold hoop in his ear. "I bet."

"Mickey."

But he wanted to push it, wanted us to go this way so he could be mad. He loved being mad. He said, "The trouble with you is, you see everything as a viable option."

Mickey started off a lot of sentences like that. He wanted to be cutting. But I liked that idea, that everything was a viable option. "What's wrong with that?" I asked him. He was already walking away, his shoulders hunched and his hands jammed into his pockets.

The earring man lost no time. He bought me a beer and we sat on the patio. Chili-pepper lights were strung overhead, casting a pink glow. His name was Ted, and by the end of the night I had kissed him, leaning against the hood of his pickup, like prom night or something. Everybody has pickups out here. His hair, which was black and looked coarse and scraggly, turned out to be soft— so soft I kept touching it. "I have to go," I kept saying. "I better go home."

Mickey was asleep when I got back. I smelled of beer and cigarettes. I brushed my teeth and pulled on a T-shirt. Mickey raised up on one elbow as I lay down in bed. In the streetlight glow I could see his brittle eyes. I had loved him, maybe, for about one day. I remembered the day. We were at his parents' house, in the country. His parents liked me. I'm a nice girl. The parents always like me. After dinner Mickey and I went for a walk. The road had tall trees on either side. We both had the same thought, that maybe we'd be taking walks like this, on this same road, in twenty years. Instead, we were having this conversation.

"Did you fuck him?"

"No. Jesus, Mickey."

"What, then? Did you kiss him?" He could see how my upper lip and chin were rubbed raw. He raised his fist.

"Don't hit me," I said. I couldn't go to my interview with a black eye. I had one dress, and I could see it hanging on the closet door. I had ironed it that afternoon. I imagined myself in it, instead of in this bed. He had never hit me before. No one had. But we had gotten ourselves into this drama. He drew his fist back further and in the dim light I could see the pale skin stretched across his ribs, his bare chest, the tuft of blond hair in his armpit. His eyes were bright as glass, his face plastic-looking in the dim light.

"I have that interview tomorrow." I was lying on Miss Piggy sheets and imploring him in this way.

He got out of bed. Got dressed, slammed the door. He'd walk, all night probably. I went to sleep. In the morning the alarm woke me. Mickey was sleeping on the couch. I took my shower, put on the dress and a pair of sandals, some makeup. My face was thin. I had lost weight on this Missouri plan.

I got the job as a receptionist for an accounting firm. I spent my first paycheck on clothes. They had a strict dress code, the women had to wear dresses, the men ties, which they loosened as soon as they arrived in the morning. Sometimes Ted picked me up for lunch. He took me to a dark steak house where Mickey would never think to go. We sat next to each other in a back booth. He smoked a cigarette with one hand and touched me under the table with the other. I excused myself, went to the ladies' room, put my panties in my purse. Things moved quickly along. I stayed over at Ted's and sneaked into the basement apartment for underwear, pantyhose, shoes. My plan was to move out, maybe be with Ted. But it wasn't so simple. Ted wasn't quite divorced from his wife. He was *almost* divorced, he said, as if it were a process totally out of his hands, like being *almost* bald. The almost-ex-wife lived in Kansas City. I couldn't move in with him, because things could get complicated for him legally if she found out.

I slipped into the apartment when I thought Mickey would be at work, but the painting jobs were erratic and sometimes he was home, watching TV, red-faced, feverish-looking. He'd press me into a corner. I could see the tiny dots of paint on his pale eyelashes. "Just one more time." Begging me for sex. "Come on, Angie. Please." While Ted was a languorous lover who stretched out our sex with breaks, Mickey was the insistent, prodding kind, rubbing himself against me in his nylon running shorts, anger and hurt in his eyes but also this heavy-breathing horniness. I gave in just so I could get out of there. After a few times like that, I hated him.

TED LIVED IN A RANCH HOUSE with a dishwasher and central air that he blasted all summer long. I was always finding his wife's stuff everywhere. A cardigan sweater hung in the closet, a ratty yellow thing I wore sometimes when I got cold. A dried-out mascara had rolled under the dresser. A crinkled tube of Monistat cream was in the medicine cabinet. She was not completely gone, that wife.

I had three dresses now that I alternated at work: a light pink one with a white collar, a black one that looked like two pieces but was just one, and a navy and white stripe, rayon, with a shiny belt. I bought a fourth one, a red knit, to wear when I asked my boss for a raise. I had a JCPenney credit card now. The day I got my raise, I stopped at Mickey's, packed up my suitcases, left the key on the table. As I pulled out of the driveway, his cousin's truck was coming down the street.

Lots of apartments were available during the summer. The college students didn't come back until the end of August. The apartment I moved into was a dream. I could barely afford it. Wall-to-wall carpeting, fresh paint, a new stove. It was the first place I had on my own. I bought a hibachi. Ted and I grilled steaks. The patio overlooked a small pool in the middle of the apartment complex, and sometimes we went swimming at night. We drank vodka and strung Christmas lights around the glass door and danced. Ted spent the night with me more and more often. He got phone calls at my place. He left some evenings to meet people. Ted worked as a custodian, cleaning churches at night. Methodists on Tuesdays, Presbyterians on Wednesdays, Baptists on Thursdays and Fridays. But he had this other business on the side. A light trade, he called it. Middle-aged hippies with a stubborn marijuana habit. I pretended not to know what was going on. I loved his wild-boy grin, and the way he danced, swinging me around. He had great arms.

MY SISTER AND I TALKED ON THE PHONE. Carol was twenty-five now and living in Delaware. She was going to physical therapy school. She worked part-time at a clinic, learning her trade.

"You just need to pick something, Angie," she told me. "It

doesn't really matter what." In the background I could hear Carol's roommate talking in a high-pitched voice to the cat.

I was sitting on the couch, Ted's head in my lap. He was smoking a cigarette and reading a race car magazine. The ashtray was balanced on his stomach. He never eavesdropped. It didn't interest him all that much, what other people were saying. He had amazing concentration. He could read in a room full of people and not even notice they were there.

"Do you like being a physical therapist?"

"The money will be good. I'll always have a job, wherever I go." She blew cigarette smoke into the mouthpiece.

"Where are you going?"

"That's not the point. If I go somewhere. Plus, you meet interesting people. I've got a date with a patient tonight."

"You're allowed to date the patients?"

Carol laughed. "Nobody cares."

"What's wrong with him?"

"What do you mean?"

"I mean, what's physically wrong with your date, that he needs therapy? Did he get hurt hang gliding?"

"He fell. It was dark. He couldn't see, and he fell."

I loved my sister but she only gave me parts of the story. "So how's our mother?"

"Batty as ever. I talked to her last week, in fact. She asked about you. 'Where's Angie? She hasn't called me in two years.'" Carol imitated her voice perfectly.

"That's a lie." But it wasn't. There wasn't any point in calling our mother.

We hung up. I felt depressed. I wondered whether being a physical therapist and dating a guy who fell down in the dark was a better life than the one I had. I didn't think physical therapy school was for me. I started putting Ted's hair into spiky little braids. He'd let me do anything to him.

"Why don't we go to your place anymore?" I asked. Carol's

phone call had irritated me. I wanted to pick a fight.

"Your place is cleaner."

"We could clean your house."

"Your place is safer."

"What?" I tugged on a braid.

"I have reason to believe that a member of the local constabulary is watching my place right now." Ted talked like this, in this quaint way. He called a couch a "divan." He used words like "fetching" to describe pretty girls. He called what we were doing "courting."

"What are you talking about? The police?"

"Nothing's going to happen. They've known about me for years. 'Ted Stippel, narcotics trafficker.' They love that I take care of the oldsters, leave the middle schoolers alone. Every once in a while they put on a tough act, shut me down for a few days. We just need to lie low."

He went back to his magazine. I got up, shifting his head to a pillow. I plugged in the Christmas lights. I had worn the ex-wife's sweater home one night, and I put it on now to go outside. It didn't seem to bother Ted that I wore her sweater. I kept waiting for him to say something about it. In one of the pockets I had found an old Bic lighter. I carried it around with me in my pocket, something to fiddle with. I went out onto the patio. I had never seen a picture of Ted's wife. Her name was Rita, but I had no idea what she looked like. A few brown leaves floated in the pool. It was late September already. I had lived here four months. I took the lighter out and clicked it, but it was almost out of fluid and only made feeble sparks. I would be twenty-two on my next birthday. I had traveled a thousand miles. I had lived with two men. I counted everything up. Then I went inside, where Ted had fallen asleep. I saw the apartment the way you would see it if you didn't live there. Beige carpet, white walls, small room. Man sleeping on couch. I put my clothes out for work the next day and went to bed.

IN OCTOBER, WE WENT TO A BAR where they had a band. Ted left our table to do some business in the parking lot. The lying low was over. Mickey was at the bar, and I was startled to see him because I thought he had gone back to Pennsylvania. He was dancing with a red-haired girl. I watched them and could tell they had just met. I knew he could fall in love with her before their dance ended—that's how he was. When the music stopped she went back to her friends, like at a high school dance. She probably was in high school, and in the bar illegally. Mickey walked over to my table.

"So where's your druggie friend?"

This town, it was too small. "He's not a druggie."

"A dealer who doesn't do drugs?" Mickey still had the page-boy, but his bangs were too short now. He squinted at me. "I hear he's dabbling in the cocaine market now."

I started to argue with him but realized he was probably right.

Sometimes I lie in my bed and with closed eyes I go back to all the other beds I have slept in. I picture where the closet would be, the bedside table, the window. I pretend I'm lying in my sister's bed, or I'm in the apartment I rented with some friends after high school, or in my grandmother's house. It's a going-to-sleep trick I play, but sometimes I get stuck. I forget where I am. Even opening my eyes doesn't always help. That was how I felt standing there with Mickey.

"You know what the trouble with you is?"

"Yes," I said.

He laughed, as if to say, Okay, you win. "You want to dance? For old times' sake?"

"All right."

It was a fast song. Mickey jumped up and down. He shook his hair. It made me laugh. He didn't really need me there at all. But his abandon was a relief—it meant he wasn't paying much attention to me. I kicked off my shoes. The dance floor wasn't full, maybe a dozen people, and I got right up near the stage, with Mickey hopping up and down, pogo-style. I was wearing a gauzy black skirt and the sheer cloth inhaled and exhaled around my legs. The drummer had his eye on me. Drummers are usually nuts. Most people would go for the lead guitarist, even the bass player, but for me the drummer was always the one to dance for. Then Ted came back. He walked up to Mickey and pushed him in the chest. That was just what Mickey wanted. They started pushing each other all over the dance floor. The lead singer was talking into the microphone, "Hey man, you're a lover, not a fighter." But it was too late. Mickey was a scrappy fighter, Viking blood; you could tell he'd fight dirty, given the chance. Ted was too messed up, though normally I would've bet on him, those arms. They were both throwing punches, not connecting much. They fell into a table, knocked over some chairs. I stood to the side feeling that weird displaced bedroom thing. A couple of bouncers pulled them apart. I walked out the back door onto the fire escape. You could sit out there if you wanted some fresh air, which I did. I could hear the singer saying they were going to take a short break.

It didn't take long for the drummer to come out for a cigarette. "You the cause of all that commotion?" He was smiling at me. He looked older than he had looked onstage.

I had the ex-wife's lighter in my hand. He gestured toward it, an unlit Marlboro held between his teeth.

"Sorry. It doesn't work."

"Just carry it around for luck, do you?" He found a book of matches in his pocket.

"You guys sound good," I said.

"Gonna have to quit soon. Can't keep up this lifestyle."

"No," I agreed.

The view from the fire escape was pretty. The bar was on the second floor, and the building itself was on a hill, so we could see the streets and trees and traffic lights, the grids of buildings and parking lots. I knew, if I wanted to, that I could complicate matters further, and throw myself in the drummer's general direction. I had suggested as much, while dancing. It was the reason he was out there.

"I think I'm going home," I said.

"Stay for one more set. We're going to do some Stevie Ray."

This was before Stevie Ray Vaughan's plane crash. He was at the height of his popularity, with bands in places like Missouri covering his songs. So much was about to happen. I didn't know that, of course. Didn't know Ted's trouble would include me for a while, didn't know I would end up with a baby and no child support, didn't know it was already too late to make a plan.

I shook Rita's lighter, flicked it once. A small flame popped up, then went out. A police car pulled up to the front of the bar.

"Looks like your friends are on their way out." The drummer laughed, shook his head, took one more drag off his cigarette before stepping on it. "Come find me, if you change your mind. I'll buy you a drink."

"Thanks," I said.

His feet clanged up the metal stairs. I remembered his face when he played, how he got that ecstatic look. I tapped the lighter against the railing. Inside, the band started up, a mumble of words, then the first chords of "Love Struck Baby." I threw the lighter as hard as I could into the black sky. I waited to see what I would do. I took my time. I was still young.

# still life

Rosemary, sixty-seven years old and an hour early at the airport, had plenty of time to think, and what she thought was: Maybe I have always been losing David. Even her pregnancy with him all those years ago had been difficult. In the third month her doctor had ordered bed rest. It was during this time that her husband, an aerial photographer for the state of New Hampshire, had first been unfaithful. She lay awake in their apartment, two fans blowing warm summer air around the bedroom, trying to read or sleep, thinking of creative ways to lure Martin home. Being pregnant with their first child wasn't, apparently, enough.

David's birth had been difficult, too. The doctors couldn't stop her bleeding. She remembered seeing the sheets and thinking, how strange, to use red sheets in a hospital. Looking up at Martin she had noted genuine concern, but all she could think was, maybe it would be better if I died. But she didn't die. She stopped bleeding, recovered slowly, and fell in love with her new baby, even through his colicky nights, even when he wouldn't nurse and she had to feed him formula—which everyone used back then anyway—and she rocked him and sang to him and she fought for her marriage. "Is it over with her?" she asked Martin one night, over pork chops and apple rings and the baby's cries. "It's over," he said, wiping his eyes with the napkin she had placed on the table for him, not knowing, when she placed it there, whether he'd be home for dinner. "Do you promise?" she asked him, dry-eyed, because in some deep part of herself she didn't care, she just wanted to know so she could figure out what to do, move back to Boston, get a job, find a babysitter. Martin nodded, and she believed him. Foolishly, as it turned out, because it wasn't over. It wasn't ever over. It went on for years, with different women, for different lengths of time. But it went on.

The difficult baby grew into a difficult toddler, throwing epic tantrums in the A&P, banging his head against his crib, biting his own forearms until they were dotted with alarming welts. In school he did poorly, though he was smart and tested well. One teacher suggested that David might be depressed. Rosemary looked at her older son who did seem depressed, and looked at her younger one who was never depressed, and wondered what had made the difference. Now, there would be intervention, Rosemary thought, as she studied the airport monitors for the information she already knew. Now, there would be referrals and therapy and a diagnosis and perhaps even medication. But back then, he was just a troubled child, and no one knew how to help him.

By the time Martin left, Rosemary was worn out. When David withdrew, spending most of his teenage years in his room with the door shut, she let him. He left home as soon as he finished high school, got married soon after. Too young, Rosemary thought, but hoped that Michelle could fix him somehow—could make him happy. Maybe then he would welcome Rosemary back into his life. Instead, he shut her out even further. By the time her grandson Austin was born, Rosemary could count on one hand the number of times she'd visited her son and his wife. "I have my own family now, Ma," David explained, as if the new family rendered the old one irrelevant.

Then David was diagnosed.

Rosemary had, by this time, moved to Florida, where she now searched the relentlessly blue sky for signs of David and Austin's plane. They were coming for a week-long visit—at Rosemary's invitation and expense—because Austin wanted to see the Magic Kingdom. Of course it was for Austin. David never would have come otherwise. Under these new, terrifying circumstances, the trip had already been postponed twice. Now it was May, already too hot, but they didn't dare wait any longer.

DAVID AND AUSTIN WERE THE LAST PASSENGERS off the plane. Rosemary wanted to rush forward and hold them both, to surround them and carry them protected through the world. For surely people were cruel. Stared, pointed, hushed their children's questions, why does that man look like that, Mommy, what's wrong with that boy's daddy? David was not just bald, but hairless—no eyebrows, no eyelashes—and his face was bloated from the chemicals, round and pale as a moon. Dark smudges circled his eyes like bruises. Except for the huge face he was just bones. "Honey," she finally said, reaching out her trembling hands. "My goodness, you must be exhausted." He tolerated a brief embrace. She bent down to ask Austin about the flight.

"It was fine," David answered. "Austin, say hi to Grandma." But Austin just ducked behind his father, clutching a baggy pant leg and hiding his face.

"That's okay. We have lots of time to get re-acquainted."

They walked slowly to the baggage area. Two pieces of luggage remained from David's flight, circling aimlessly. Rosemary recognized the blue Samsonite she and Martin had given to David on his fourteenth birthday, a month, as it turned out, before Martin left. She grabbed the suitcase, which felt surprisingly light but still too heavy for David to carry. The duffel bag behind it was covered with stickers, characters from a popular cartoon series. She took it too, waving away David's perfunctory gesture of assistance. "Who's your favorite guy?" she asked Austin, and he began explaining his hierarchy of preferences. Rosemary, who knew something about the show from her neighbor's son, was able to keep the conversation going until they got to the car.

"I had no idea you were so well informed," David said as he eased himself into the passenger seat. A film of sweat coated his face. She wished she'd parked closer.

"Well, you've got to keep up with these things." She patted David's bony leg. "Are you okay?"

"You mean, aside from being riddled with cancer? Yeah, great."

"No, I meant—"

"What's the riddle, Daddy?"

Rosemary pulled the car into the airport traffic. "The riddle is, what's a ghost's favorite dessert?"

"I don't know, what?"

"Booberry pie and I scream!"

Austin and David groaned and laughed. Then it was quiet and Austin said, "No, you said a riddle about cancer, Daddy."

David turned around to look at Austin. "Did I? Well, let's not worry about it right now."

Rosemary glanced at David, but he was looking at the ugliness along I-4, his teeth clenching and unclenching. She drove badly, stopping and starting in jerky motions.

"I'm going to throw up back here," Austin complained.

"I'm sorry, honey. I guess I'm just nervous."

"What are you nervous about?" David asked. His voice was calm, but with an edge of contempt.

"Oh—just nervous. Just wanting everything to go well."

"Ma. Quit worrying. We're here, aren't we?" He turned to Austin again. "We're here, aren't we, Bud?"

"Yup. We're here, Daddy."

Rosemary forced herself to loosen her grip on the steering wheel, to relax her jumpy foot. We're here.

ROSEMARY SERVED THE SIMPLE SUPPER she spent the last week planning: chicken salad, sliced strawberries, steamed green beans, rolls, and homemade brownies for dessert. She rarely cooked anymore, so it pleased her to busy herself in the kitchen again, to chop celery, trim beans, fold dough into crescent shapes, melt unsweetened chocolate squares and butter together. Austin ate everything on his plate, even asked for seconds, but David hardly touched his food. "It's the scar tissue," Austin explained, when David excused himself to go lie down. "From the radiation treatments. He can't swallow so good."

Rosemary nodded. "What does he like eating at home?"

"Mom doesn't really have time to cook. Usually we get tacos or pizza or McDonald's. Dad eats oatmeal from the microwave or sometimes I make him that instant kind of vanilla pudding."

Rosemary nodded again, and went through an inventory of soft foods she could make for her son: protein milk shakes, pureed soups, mashed potatoes. She washed the dishes while Austin lay in front of the TV watching a tape she had rented for him. He was a good boy, no matter what was going on at home. He had brought his plate to the kitchen. He made pudding for his daddy. The thought of all that junk food made Rosemary shudder. She put the leftovers in bowls and covered them with plastic wrap, thinking of how she might move back to New Hampshire, at least for the summer. She could cook meals and do errands and laundry; she could help with Austin. Of course, there was the problem of Michelle. Michelle who screamed and slammed doors during arguments, hung up on people she was angry with, spent one Thanksgiving dinner locked in the bathroom, and cashed birthday checks but never thanked the person who sent them. Rosemary sighed and made herself a cup of coffee. No point in going over that old ground. She checked on Austin, who was clutching a pale yellow square of soft faded flannel that looked ready for the dust-rag bag. He was surreptitiously sucking his thumb. Rosemary stepped outside onto her terrace without disturbing him.

Rosemary's favorite thing about Florida was her terrace: her thriving bougainvillea, the pot of herbs she grew for her salads, the sycamore canopy above, the courtyard below. She watched her neighbor's son throwing a tennis ball in the air and catching it, over and over. He had troubles too, a single mother who worked a night shift, a learning disability. Rosemary closed her eyes and listened to the occasional shouts and squeals coming from the TV. Tomorrow she would take her son and grandson to the Magic Kingdom. She would miss the drawing class she was taking at the community center nearby, but she didn't mind. They were working on still lifes. Rosemary's last bowl of fruit had not turned out the way she planned: the apples were flat, the bananas skinny and distorted. Still, she enjoyed her classmates, game senior citizens always joking about their efforts, and she loved the teacher, Chloe, a young woman with degrees in art and gerontology, who wore her hair in a long blond braid and laughed easily. Chloe was teaching them about positive and negative space, how you have to pay attention not just to the objects you draw but to the space surrounding the objects, how shapes exist even where there is nothing. She had them draw a hard-backed chair by concentrating on the empty places between the slats. Now Rosemary tried to see negative space everywhere—between the palm leaves, between the cars in the parking lot, between the lamp and the end table in her living room. She thought she could almost do it.

"I guess I'll turn in now," a voice behind her said. David. She started, and remembered how the boys used to love sneaking up on her, jumping out from behind chairs or doors. When she turned to David now, he was smiling, and she smiled back. "You startled me," she said. He nodded, his head bobbing, balloon-like.

Inside, Austin lay on the floor, sleeping. David stood awkwardly, waiting for something. "There are fresh towels on the rack in your bathroom, and an extra blanket in the closet in your room. Is there anything else I can get you?"

"No, everything's fine. It's just—" he motioned toward Austin.

"What is it, David?"

He looked at her in frustration, the circles under his eyes almost black. His arms fell to his sides. "I can't pick him up, Ma."

"Oh, of course. I'm sorry." It took her several tries before she was able to stand up with the boy in her arms, and she could feel her back pull with the strain. "Well, he is heavy," she whispered, carrying him to the guest room.

"Is he?"

Rosemary lay Austin on the bed. "Yes. He is. And beautiful, too." She kissed his forehead lightly.

"Thanks. I can take it from here." David undressed his son, moving his limbs carefully, slipping on a pair of pajama bottoms, touching him with such tenderness that Rosemary couldn't watch anymore, and said good night. She turned off the living room lights, locked the sliding glass door, and went to her room where she curled up on her bed, fully clothed, and wept.

THE NEXT MORNING ROSEMARY WOKE UP AFTER EIGHT. Panic rose in her as if she had missed an important appointment. She got out of bed so quickly she had to sit down and rest her head briefly in her hands. A piece of dream floated up to her: David in a hospital bed, except the bed was in their old living room in New Hampshire, in the farmhouse where they had all lived together. She could see the stenciling on the walls, the hooked rugs, the wooden duck near the fireplace, the aerial photograph of their house and property that Martin had framed and given to her when they first moved in. Maybe that was how he had always seen their life together—from such a long distance away it looked almost inconsequential. Just another detail in the larger landscape that was his real home.

In the dream David was happy. He was dying, but he was happy. He took Rosemary's hand and put it on his belly. She could feel a tumor there, as large as a baseball. It rolled from one side of his belly to the other. "It moves," he said to her, as if this were good news. The blankets were pulled up to his waist but the yellowish skin of his torso was exposed to her for the first time since he was a teenager, mowing the lawn in cutoffs, getting sunburned, unlike his brother whose skin in summer turned movie-star bronze. Rosemary sat on her bed, rubbing her fingers lightly together. She could still feel the tumor swimming under the surface of David's flesh. She could see him smiling, as if cancer weren't a hideous thing, killing him, but something he had come to know, even trust. *It moves.*

She put on her bathrobe and headed for the kitchen to make coffee. It was Wednesday, a good day for Disney World, and if David was willing to ride in a wheelchair (she wasn't sure he had a choice) they could advance to the head of the lines. When she got to the living room, it took her a moment to comprehend what she saw: David lying on the couch in a pair of black sweatpants and a white V-neck T-shirt, his arms crossed over his chest and a thermometer in his mouth; Austin lying under the glass coffee table, pretending to play with a matchbox car but really watching his father through the glass.

"David? Are you okay?"

He looked at her, his eyes half-opened. She felt he was saying something to her. This is all your fault. He removed the thermometer from his mouth and read it. He shook his head. "It's only one hundred." He lay his arm over his eyes.

"But with the chemotherapy—a fever could mean infection, right? We have to get you to a hospital, don't we, David?" She was sitting next to him on the couch now, her bare legs covered with goose bumps. She glanced down through the glass table. Austin was studying them, waiting, it seemed, for the disappointment he knew was going to come.

"Austin," David said. The boy turned his face away. "Austin, Daddy's sick again. I'm sorry, Bud. But you and Grandma will go see the Magic Kingdom, okay? Austin?"

"No. I don't want to go anyway. I just want to go home."

"We'll figure something out," Rosemary said.

"Goddamn it," David muttered. His voice was low and intense. "I am sick of this. I am goddamned sick of this." He pounded the sofa cushion with one fist, his face still shielded by the other arm. "Sick—to—death—"

"Hold on," Rosemary said, grabbing his hand and holding it for a moment before he pulled away. "We'll get you to the hospital. We'll see what the doctors say. Austin, we'll go to the Magic Kingdom when Daddy's feeling better."

Austin crawled up on the sofa, hiding his face in Rosemary's robe. She patted his back. "Come, let's get dressed." She made coffee and helped Austin find a clean pair of shorts in his duffel bag, then poured cereal into bowls. One foot in front of the other, she told herself. She called her own internist, then the hospital. She glanced at her watch. The drawing class was just now beginning. Chloe was probably, at that moment, assembling a still life on the table in the front of the room. What would it be this week? A bowl of oranges, perhaps, or a white pitcher on a blue tray. Rosemary brushed her hair, put on some lipstick. Maybe daisies in a jelly jar, the green stems slightly magnified in the clear water. "How might you draw this?" Chloe would ask, smiling. "Where's the negative space?" Rosemary didn't know. In front of her she imagined the heavy sheet of paper, the pencil, the eraser. She saw herself picking up the pencil to begin sketching, putting the pencil down. She could hear her own breathing, her heart beating. She wanted to say, Wait. Let me just look. She wanted to be in that room with Chloe and the things on the table, just looking.

THIS WAS THE RISK: that David would catch a cold or pick up an infection while his white blood cell count was so low from his final round of chemotherapy that his body couldn't put up a fight. A temperature above normal, even just a hundred degrees, meant another hospitalization, another IV.

After spending the day getting David admitted, Rosemary and Austin sat on her terrace eating burgers and fries. In the courtyard below, the neighbor's boy was again tossing his tennis ball. Rosemary watched Austin watching the boy. Did he want to go down and play? Did he need her to introduce the two of them? Austin dipped a French fry in ketchup, bit it in half, chewed slowly. "Is that a palm tree?" he asked, pointing. Rosemary nodded. "I've never seen one before." She nodded again; she couldn't speak. The tasks of the day, the waiting, the signing of papers, the grim resignation on David's face, had worn her out. She thought of Michelle, working full time in a Realtor's office, coming home every night to a sick husband. What did they talk about? Did they still scream and fight, or had they found a new tenderness with each other? David hadn't mentioned Michelle since he arrived. He hadn't even called her.

The next morning, as Austin finished his cereal, David called from the hospital. They talked for a while. Austin said okay and uh-huh, and smiled a few times. When he got off the phone Austin told Rosemary he wanted to go to the Magic Kingdom with her after all, and visit his father on the way home. So that was what they did. They went on the Swiss Family Robinson ride, It's a Small World (which even Austin found corny), and the pirate ship. They watched the parade, met Goofy, ate corn dogs and cotton candy, bought Mickey and Minnie nightshirts for David and Michelle. When they came to Space Mountain, Austin looked up. "What's that?" he asked.

"I think it's a roller coaster. Only it's in the dark, like outer space—"

"That sounds awesome. Let's go on it, Grandma! Come on!"

"Oh Austin, I'm too old. I was too old thirty years ago, and I'm really too old now. You go on it, and I'll wait for you right here."

"No! You come with me. It'll be so cool. Please? Please, Grandma?" He jumped up and down, pleading, until Rosemary finally gave in. "I cannot believe I'm doing this," she said when they reached the front of the line. A young man put the safety bar over them. The train of cars inched ominously forward. "Oh my god, I can't believe I'm doing this," she said again, while Austin laughed. The cars crawled up the track and into a long cold dark tunnel. Illuminated planets dangled in the artificial sky. It was beautiful and frightening. The cars climbed the track and then plunged down through the blackness. Rosemary and Austin screamed and giggled and gripped each other's hands on the safety bar. When the ride was done, they stepped out of the car on rubbery legs, and limped toward a bench. The warm humid air washed over them. Rosemary gave Austin money to buy sodas. They rested there, sipping cold drinks and watching other tired people straggling by.

"I haven't done anything like that since your daddy was a little boy."

"Did he like roller coasters when he was little?"

"Oh, he loved them. He and your uncle Rick could ride them all day, if I let them."

"He couldn't ride one now, though. If he'd come with us, he couldn't have gone on that ride with me."

Rosemary started to object, to say, Well, when Daddy's better. Austin was waiting. She met his gaze. "No," she said. "You're right. He's too sick right now."

**still life**      153

Austin nodded. He slurped the last of his drink.

"You know, Austin, you can come see me whenever you want."

He looked up at her. "You mean, if Daddy dies."

Rosemary caught her breath. She put her arm around the boy, who could have been her own son, the same cowlick, the same long eyelashes, the same dark eyes and full lower lip.

"Yes," she said finally. "That's what I mean."

AT THE HOSPITAL, DAVID WAS SLEEPING. Rosemary bought Austin two comic books at the gift shop, and a small toy plane with decals on the wings. She left him in David's room while she found a pay phone down the hall. She dialed Martin's number. Jane, the third wife, answered.

"Hi, Rosemary," she said, perfectly friendly. Of course, there was no reason not to be. They hadn't overlapped. "I'm sorry, Marty's not here. Could I have him call you back?" In the background Rosemary could hear jazz playing on the stereo. Dave Brubeck, she guessed.

"It's all right. I'm at the hospital, in Orlando. David's been admitted."

"My god, is everything okay?"

"Yes. Well, no. He has a fever. They've got him on antibiotics. He couldn't go with us, with Austin and me, to Disney World. I'm sorry—I just wanted to talk to Martin."

"He should be back any minute. Rosemary, I don't know what to say. This whole thing. It's just so hard. It's tearing Marty apart, he hardly sleeps at night."

They talked for a few minutes, Rosemary imagining their house in Richmond, and thinking again about how Jane was just a year older than David, and though she was nice enough, she simply had no idea. She thought she could imagine what all this was like, but she was wrong.

When Rosemary returned to David's room, he was awake. Austin was curled up on his bed, expertly avoiding the IV side. He was playing with the plane, flying it around David's head and landing it gently on his chest. When he saw Rosemary he said, "Can I tell her now, Dad?" David nodded. "Daddy bet me that you wouldn't ride on Space Mountain, and I won the bet."

Rosemary laughed. "Ah, so that's what you were up to. What did you win?"

"This—" Austin pulled up David's hospital gown to expose his belly, and blew a loud raspberry in the middle of his pale flesh, and then another one, sputtering and giggling, while David cried out in a mock squeal, "No, no, please stop!" Austin collapsed next to him, sighing and holding his hand. A fragment from Rosemary's dream floated up to her: the itinerant, almost whimsical tumor, and David's peace with it.

"You should've seen Grandma on that ride."

"Yeah?"

"She screamed her head off!"

"I'll bet." David smiled.

"And she said I can come back to see her, and maybe we could do the Space Mountain ride again."

"Sure." He kissed Austin on the head, and looked at Rosemary, his eyes telegraphing a quick thank you. But mostly what she saw in them was the pure wild love a parent feels for a child. And, she knew, the same look was reflected back to him.


DAVID WAS DISCHARGED FROM THE HOSPITAL the day before he and Austin were to leave. His color was better, Rosemary thought, and she felt encouraged when he ate most of the meal she had prepared—cream of broccoli soup, cheese soufflé, strawberry sorbet. After dinner Rosemary took Austin next door and introduced him to her neighbor's son, and the two boys ran down to the courtyard to play. Rosemary and David sat on the terrace, the first time they'd been alone since he arrived. He sipped a can of vanilla Ensure while Rosemary drank her coffee. They watched the two boys devise a game of tag. It had a complicated set of rules involving the palm trees, the condominium's mailboxes, and the sidewalk.

"David, I've been thinking," Rosemary began. She put her coffee cup down and looked at her son. "I want to come up to New Hampshire for the summer. I can stay with old friends, or find a rental. It's too hot here anyway. And I want to help, any way you need me to. Cooking, shopping, laundry, you name it."

David nodded. He was leaning back in the chaise longue, still watching Austin, his white hands forming a bridge for his chin, as if his head were too heavy to hold up. Rosemary wondered if he had heard her. Finally he said, "I think it's a good idea. But you should know that Michelle—"

Rosemary broke in, prepared for this. "I know Michelle doesn't want me up there, but she has to understand—"

"No. That's not what I was going to say. I was going to say that you should know: Michelle is having an affair." He looked at her, and his forehead wrinkled as he raised his invisible eyebrows, as if to say, how do you like that.

"Oh, David—"

"No. Don't start. It's all right. It's been going on for a while. Even before I got sick."

"I'm so sorry, honey."

"Yeah, well. We were never exactly a match made in heaven. Should've quit years ago. But then Austin came along."

"Children change things."

"They change everything."

"Yes."

"Did I change things, for you and Dad?" He kept looking at the boys below, as if embarrassed by his own question.

Rosemary started, unprepared for his directness. They had never spoken of the divorce, of the marriage before the children, of the slow dissolution over the years. "Of course. Yes. But some things no one could change."

"Dad's cheating."

"Yes, that. Other things, too. I'm not sure … Martin and I could ever really connect. Not in any real way." Rosemary struggled for words. "That was my fault too. I guess I withdrew. So. We had some nice times. We had two beautiful children, and that was the best part. It all seems like such a long time ago now. I hardly know what it was like to live that life."

"I do. I know."

Rosemary looked in her son's face, the wide-open eyelashless eyes, the wispy bits of hair on his skull, colorless wisps like a baby's. The little boys' voices bounced around in the balmy evening air. The truth was, she didn't want to go any further into this. But David was there, sitting next to her, waiting.

"What's it like, then?" she asked softly.

He smiled. Took a sip of his drink. Kept his eyes on Austin as he spoke. "It's like this. You're sitting, like this, after dinner say, having a cup of coffee together," he lifted the Ensure in a self-mocking gesture. "And you're glad she's sitting there because there are lots of nights she's not sitting there. She's, you know, working late or working out or visiting a friend. It's a code. You both speak in this code, pretending that you're not, pretending that everything's just as it seems."

Rosemary nodded. "I remember." And she did. The summer she was pregnant with David, she and Martin talked to each other as if they were reading from a script. Everything they said sounded hollow.

"She takes a sip of coffee and you listen to her talking to your son about his day at school or whatever. But you're wondering all the time, where is she really? In that moment, in her head, where is she? Is she kissing the guy? More? What?" David glanced at Rosemary, then away again. He pressed his fingertips to his eyelids briefly. "You can drive yourself crazy."

"That's no way to live," she said.

"I don't have much choice."

Rosemary cleared her throat. "You could leave her."

"No. We've agreed on that. We've agreed we don't want Austin to know about any of this. Michelle has promised me that she'll wait … before she gets married … at least one year—"

"Stop. Please. I can't hear this."

"Then don't." He shrugged. "What you hear is up to you." In his voice was the implication, *as usual.* "I'm simply telling you, Ma. This is how it is."

That could be Ricky and David down there, she thought, running around in circles, chasing each other. There were good times. David wasn't always unhappy. He was a little boy who built moon stations with Legos and collected Matchbox cars, and he was a teenager who listened to the Allman Brothers and wore tie-dyed shirts and once he came up behind her in the kitchen when he was eleven or twelve and gave her a hug, just like that. In the summer they'd eat spareribs and corn from the farmers' market at the picnic table in the backyard, and the children would do all the usual things, catch fireflies, throw a baseball around, lie on the grass and look at stars. Times like that. Ordinary times. They were a family. And then: Was it true? Did she only hear what she wanted to hear? Were there things she should have heard, and didn't? She looked at her son. She looked at the negative space between them, the shape it made, its angles and contours. She could see it plainly, how large and open a thing it was, how sharp in places and then rounded, soft, an arc that she could stick her hand right through.

"Okay," Rosemary said. "This is how it is."

David looked at her, surprised, as if she had just walked onto the terrace and not been sitting there all along. "Okay," he said. And they stayed together like that, her hand resting on his arm, watching evening spread over the courtyard, thinking of the summer nights to come.